blue
rider
press

TRAVELING
SPRINKLER

BLUE RIDER PRESS · *a member of Penguin Group (USA)* · *New York*

TRAVELING SPRINKLER

a novel

NICHOLSON

BAKER

blue
rider
press

Published by the Penguin Group
Penguin Group (USA) LLC
375 Hudson Street
New York, New York 10014

USA · Canada · UK · Ireland · Australia
New Zealand · India · South Africa · China

penguin.com
A Penguin Random House Company

Library of Congress Cataloging-in-Publication Data

Baker, Nicholson.
Traveling sprinkler / Nicholson Baker.
p.   cm.
ISBN 978-0-399-16096-7
1. Poets—Fiction. 2. Man-woman relationships—Fiction. I. Title.
PS3552.A4325T73   2013   2013019296
813'.54—dc23

Printed in the United States of America
1   3   5   7   9   10   8   6   4   2

Book design by Michelle McMillian

To M.

One

R OZ CALLED TO ASK ME what I wanted for my fifty-fifth birthday. One of her many good qualities is that she remembers people's birthdays. I thought for a second. I knew what I wanted: I wanted a cheap acoustic guitar. You can get them for about seventy dollars at Best Buy. They come in an exciting cardboard box. I saw two boxes, leaning against a wall, waiting, last time I was there. I almost said that's what I wanted—I came dangerously close to saying it—but then I didn't, because you really can't ask your former girlfriend for a guitar, even a cheap guitar. It's too momentous a present. It presupposes too much. It puts her in an awkward position. And of course you can't say, "What I really want is I want you back," either.

So instead I said, "I think what I really want is an egg

salad sandwich." Roz has a particular way with egg salad—
she adds in a rare kind of paprika or tarragon or some elusive
spice I don't understand. "We could meet at Fort McClary,"
I said. "I'll bring the picnic basket and the sliced carrots if
you bring the egg salad sandwiches."

Fort McClary is a place we used to go sometimes to smell
the seaweed and look at the boats. I think it's where the
Revolutionary War began, but I'm not sure. There are huge
hewn Stonehengeian stones tumbled about in the grass that
were going to be part of a defensive wall that never got built.
I think Paul Revere rode his poor snorting horse all the way
to Fort McClary to warn that the British were coming, which
was the beginning of a pointless trade war that didn't need to
happen.

Roz was silent for a moment.

"Or," I said, "if a picnic is too heavy-duty we could just
have lunch at the Friendly Toast."

"No, no, I can definitely make you an egg salad sandwich,"
she said. I could hear her smiling the indulgent smile of
someone who once loved somebody a long time ago.

We agreed to meet at Fort McClary and have a birthday
picnic.

EARLY THIS MORNING I had a literary dream. Roz was
still living with me and I was supposed to review a book of
military recipes called *Mess: Great Food from Army Kitchens*.
Roz and I were testing one of the recipes, which was for

octopus-walnut muffins. Roz pulled the tray of muffins out of the oven and I bit into one. "How does it taste?" she asked.

"Not too good," I said.

"I'm not surprised," she said. We shook our heads and tried to think of a way I could say something nice about the cookbook.

"Maybe you could praise the walnuts?" Roz said.

I woke up.

I'M PARKED ON INIGO ROAD, which is my favorite road anywhere. I wish I could write about the phrase "happy phrase," but there's no time. Very soon I'm going to be Fifty Fucking Five. The three Fs. The last time I hit three Fs was ten years ago, and this time is definitely worse. Unless you're Yeats or Merwin you are done as a poet at fifty-five. Dylan Thomas was in the ground for sixteen years at fifty-five. Keats was dead at, what, twenty-six? Riding on horseback with his sad lungs coughing blood. And as for Wilfred Owen.

The first time I read Keats's sonnet "When I Have Fears," I was eating a tuna sub. I was an applied music major, with a concentration in bassoon. I'd found the poem in *The Norton Anthology of Poetry*—the shorter black edition with the Blake watercolor of a griffin on the cover. I propped the Norton open with my brown plastic food tray and I started reading and eating the tuna sub and drinking V8 juice occasionally from a little can.

Keats says: "When I have fears that I may cease to be." He

doesn't say, "When I have fears that I may," you know, "drop dead," or "breathe my last"—no, it's "cease to be." I stopped chewing. I was caught by the emptiness and ungraspability in that phrase. And then came the next line, and I made a little hum of amazement: "When I have fears that I may cease to be," Keats says, "Before my pen has gleaned my teeming brain."

I don't want to pretend that the cafeteria spun around. It stayed still. I heard the grinding sound of the cash register printing. But I was thinking very hard. I was thinking about a large tortoiseshell that somebody had given me when I was small. There was a sort of fused backbone on the inside of it that ran down the middle. This bony ridge smelled terrible when you sniffed it close-up, although it had no odor from a normal distance. I imagined the tortoiseshell as the top dome of a human skull, and I imagined Keats's pen gleaning bits of thought flesh from it.

The pen is really the only tool sharp enough to do the job of brain-gleaning properly. Keats knew that. He had medical training. He was supposed to be a doctor. He didn't like medical school much, but he assisted at surgeries. The idea of the inside of the head as an object that had crevices and hiding places—that it was gleanable—was something that he knew firsthand. And he also knew, because he was a sick man, that his fears were justified. His mother died of consumption. He was a fourteen-year-old boy when he stayed up watching her die. He knew what it meant for a complicated gentle person to simply cease to be. And his brain was teeming with the unwrittenness of what he had to say. He had to hurry. He knew all that.

The rest of the poem isn't nearly so good, but it ends with a bang: "Till Love and Fame to nothingness do sink."

I DIDN'T BRING the list of things I wanted to write about today. Sometimes I note things I want to write about on a folded piece of paper, but I left my piece of paper in my bed. It's an empty bed. This may be one of the empty-bed birthdays. I've had a few.

But a summer birthday is a good thing. On the branch near my car, on every twig that isn't dead, there has been a lot of activity. The sap is up in these trees, and the leaves have had no choice but to move outward. Billions of buds in each tree, the leaves tremblingly uncurving, squirming outward. It's a forced migration. The sap is pressurized and the leaves have to flee outward from the very ends of the twigs. What it creates is a fog of green over all of Inigo Road.

I've just been waiting for summer, waiting and wanting, and now it's here. Yesterday was actually hot, and today I've put a Post-it note on the corner of my computer screen: NO YUKON JACK TILL YOU FINISH. I need a new drug. Huey Lewis sang that song and then foolishly sued Ray Parker, Jr., claiming that Parker had pinched the bassline for the *Ghostbusters* theme.

I'm debating whether to buy a can of Skoal smokeless tobacco.

THREE QUICK FAREWELL SHOTS of Yukon Jack. Oh my flipping God. Deep breath now. Hello, my strangely shaped figments, I'm Paul Chowder. I'm here and so are you. We are in the same Minkowski space, shaped like a saddle. You're in the saddle and I'm in the saddle and we're not going to fall off Revere's horse because it doesn't exist.

My knees are laughing. Is that allowed?

Here's my tip of the night. Nod. It's worth nodding at things sometimes. Just give a big nod. That's the way they are? Okay, nod, yes. Practice nodding.

Thirty-five years ago, when I was twenty, I sold my Heckel bassoon. And that was that. Now I'm supposed to be writing a new book of poetry, which I'm calling *Misery Hat*. I don't want to work on it. Today, to get inspired, I dipped into an extremely long poem by Samuel Rogers called *Human Life*, because I liked the title. It didn't do much for me, but I remembered that Samuel Rogers was friends with Tennyson and Coleridge, and that made me haul out my old edition of Tennyson and look at his extremely long poem *Maud*, narrated by an insane person who rambles. Tennyson was very ill if not clinically insane when he wrote parts of *Maud*, and a lot of it is unreadable. But there is one very nice soaring patch that everyone remembers. It begins, "Come into the garden, Maud, / For the black bat, night, has flown." There Tennyson has us. Night itself is a black bat. How thrilling and un-Victorian is that? In the same passage there's a mention of an unusual chamber group that's apparently been serenading the roses all night long—a flute, a violin, and a bassoon. It's a bassoon not because Tennyson knew anything about the bassoon, but because he needed an evocative word to rhyme with "tune" and "moon." And also because he may have been remembering another poetical bassoon passage, from Coleridge's *Ancient Mariner*:

> The Wedding-Guest here beat his breast,
> For he heard the loud bassoon.

Coleridge didn't know much about the bassoon either, or he wouldn't have said it was loud. The bassoon's liability as an orchestral instrument is that it is quite soft, much softer in volume than its size would suggest. At a wedding reception in 1797, when Coleridge was working on his poem, it might have been used to double the bassline played by the spinet or the cello. But bassoonists the world over are grateful to Coleridge for including them in his stanza.

Charles Darwin knew slightly more about the bassoon than either Coleridge or Tennyson. When he was old and sad he asked his son to play bassoon for a heap of earthworms, to study their responsiveness to low sounds. He also played a tin whistle for them and pounded on the piano and shouted at them. "They took not the least notice," Darwin said. There's also a poem about the vowels by John Gould Fletcher, one of the Imagists. The letter U, according to Fletcher, sounds like "torrid bassoons and flutes that murmur without repose, / Butterflies, bumblebees, buzzing about a hot rose." Fletcher read the torrid bassoons passage to Amy Lowell in London, and later he wrote an autobiography called *Life Is My Song*. Later still, depressed, he drowned himself in less than three feet of water in a recently dredged pond in Little Rock, Arkansas.

Selling my bassoon was one of the biggest mistakes I've ever made. I've regretted it a thousand times since. And here's the strange thing. I've written three books of poems, and I've never once written a bassoon poem. I have never used the word "bassoon" in a single poem. Not once. I guess I was saving it up, which is not always a good idea.

NAN, MY NEXT-DOOR NEIGHBOR, asked me to help with her chickens. She has five hens plus one droopy-tailed bantam rooster who has a reputation for being fierce and territorial, although he's always fine with me, staring at me warily from one eye and cock-a-doodling a fair amount. Nan is away in Toronto taking care of her mother, who isn't doing well. She, Nan, has been acting a little odd recently—preoccupied and remote. It could be that she's worried about her mom, but also I think her "friend," Chuck, is maybe no longer in the picture. He takes care of submarines, and there was an arson fire at the Navy base in Kittery that caused half a billion dollars' worth of damage to a very fancy nuclear submarine. A worker at the base confessed to setting the fire because he wanted to leave early that day. That's how things are in the Navy.

All I have to do is let the chickens out in the morning, so that they can spend the day pecking for trifles in the grass. I scatter some cracked corn under the bushes to give them a better peck-to-success ratio. Then, as dusk comes, I wait for them to file back into their shed and I close the door. You can't herd them, you just have to wait till they go in of their own accord. I've gotten in the habit of bringing my white plastic chair over to Nan's yard and waiting for them to be done with their day. If I don't close the door, the chickens may be attacked at night by raccoons or foxes.

Ah, there they go now, filing into their enclosure. The hens are big and brown and fluffy, and their back parts are white with chickenshit and egg laying. The rooster is small and iridescently blue-black. I guess they mate all night, I don't know. There's a faded sign on the door that says "Every Birdie Welcome."

THE WHITE PLASTIC CHAIR is comfortable, but not as comfortable as the driver's seat of my car. I practically live in my car these days, and I usually buy gas at Irving Circle K. One reason I like Irving is that they play oldies music from tinny speakers at the gas pump. Another reason is that they leave the little clickers in the pump handle so that you can start filling your tank and then go inside to buy a bottle of Pellegrino water and a bag of Planter's trail mix from a man at the register who looks like he's nursing a massive hangover.

Today at Irving I went back out to the car with my

purchases and I absentmindedly tried to drive off without removing the gas spout from my car. I heard a clunk and looked back and saw the pump hose lying on the ground, surrounded by what seemed to be a dark spreading stain of gasoline. I thought I'd torn off the handle. I said, "Oh, no!" and got out, and then I saw that it was just a trick of the shadows. The spout was fine. It had pulled free of the car and fallen, and there was no sign of damage to the hose and no leaked gas. I felt a huge relief. I drove off singing a song that I heard a few weeks ago in Quaker meeting, called "How Can I Keep from Singing?" One of the meeting elders, Chase, had stood in the silence and said that all morning he'd been remembering a song that Pete Seeger used to sing. Pete Seeger learned it from a singer named Doris Plenn, Chase said, who learned it from her grandmother. And then he sang it. He wasn't a great singer, but it didn't matter. "My life flows on in endless song," he sang. "Above earth's lamentation." I was so impressed by the song that when I got home I looked it up on iTunes and bought two versions of it, one by Bruce Springsteen and one by a group called Cordelia's Dad, accompanied by slow fiddle chords.

Long ago the Quakers were opposed to music—they said that the effort a musician expended to learn an instrument kept him from worthier pursuits. But now they sometimes stand and sing at meeting.

I really need a guitar.

Two

I HAD LUNCH IN WALTHAM with my friend Tim at a bakery he likes. He teaches at Tufts. He's a good man, and he is truly obsessed now with killer drones. Once he could talk about nothing but Queen Victoria's war crimes, now it's Predators and Reapers and the CIA's chief of drones, John Brennan. Tim's new hero is Medea Benjamin, of CODEPINK, who's published a book called *Drone Warfare*. He's back from a drone summit in Washington, where Medea and other anti-drone people gave talks. He asked me to go with him, but I said no—it's too far, too upsetting, too awful, too current.

While Tim and I stood in line waiting to order, he told me about what happened when Medea Benjamin went to a talk that John Brennan gave. It was apparently quite a scene. Tim whipped out his phone and played me a YouTube video. Brennan is talking about Al Qaeda's killing of men, women, and children, and suddenly Medea Benjamin stands and says,

"What about the hundreds of innocent people we are killing with our drone strikes in Pakistan and in Yemen and Somalia? I speak out on behalf of those innocent victims." The woman moderator tries to quiet her, but Medea won't be silenced. A huge man with a yellow POLICE shirt on seizes her and lifts her and she's dragged out, still talking loudly about the killing of innocents and the Constitution and the rule of law. She holds on to the exit doorway, trying to stay in the room, while the huge yellow shave-headed policeman hauls at her, and she says, "I love the rule of law. I love my country. You're making us less safe by killing so many innocent people around the world, shame on you!" And then the door closes and she's taken away. Brennan adjusts the microphone, quietly says thank you to nobody in particular, and continues his address.

"Can you believe her?" said Tim.

"She's really something," I said.

We reached the front of the ordering line. "You should get the tuna and artichoke sandwich," he said. "The economics of this place escapes me. There are nine people behind the counter. They bake their own bread and they make these fantastic tuna and artichoke sandwiches."

We sat down outside and Tim asked me what I was up to. I told him that I'd been taking care of some chickens, and that I'd stopped drinking Yukon Jack because it wasn't working for me and I had to finish a book of poems. I said I was thinking of trying Skoal smokeless tobacco.

"You mean those little cans?" said Tim. "Oh God, no. If you're going down the tobacco road you should smoke a pipe. It's more your style."

"My grandfather smoked a pipe and it wasn't good for him," I said.

"What about cigars? Mark Twain was a huge cigar man. Not to mention Castro, and JFK."

"But then you have this big brown thing sticking out of your face. I don't want to be wreathed in plumes of smoke."

"I can understand that," said Tim. "But Skoal is for rednecks."

I took a bite of sandwich, thinking about cigars. "Amy Lowell smoked cigars all night," I said. "She smoked cigars and wrote poems, and boom, she was an Imagist."

"There you go," said Tim.

"But Imagism wasn't that great. Anyway I'm done with poetry."

Tim scoffed. "You're not done with poetry."

"Yes, I am. I'm going to play the guitar."

"Ah, the guitar," Tim said. "I know two, no, three people at Tufts who've taken up guitar. It's the middle-aged thing to do. At faculty parties they sneak off and play Clapton Unplugged and Blind Lemon Jefferson."

"Exactly," I said. "I want to get back to music somehow. I miss it."

"That's true, I forgot, you used to play the oboe."

"The bassoon, but yes."

"Maybe you could write songs."

"Maybe. While I was driving here I was singing a song about seaweed."

"Leanin' toward the carrageenan, eh? Any protest songs? Antiwar songs?"

"No, but I've been working on some political poems. I've got a long bad poem in the pipeline about Archibald MacLeish and the CIA."

"Sounds unwieldy." Tim wiped his mouth. "What we need is an anti-drone anthem. Something to sing on the barricades, like Dylan's 'Masters of War.'"

I asked him what he thought was the best antiwar song ever.

He considered the question, chewing. Donovan's "Universal Soldier" maybe, he thought, or Lennon's "Imagine." No, the best antiwar song, he said conclusively, was by somebody named Bagel.

I looked dubious. "The guy's name is Bagel?"

"Bogle. It's about World War One." He put down his sandwich and pulled out his phone again. "There's a great version of it on YouTube, by this young kid who just sings the hell out of it." He poked at the screen for a while, frowning, but couldn't find the video. "I'll send you the link. I guarantee you will shed a tear."

I asked Tim if he'd been on any dates. "Nothing on that front," he said. "I'm saving all my love for Medea Benjamin."

I drove back to Portsmouth, up Route 95, with my tires going around and around saying the same things to the road over and over again. The road never gets it, never learns. When I veered toward the edge of the lane, my tires drove over the intermittent white lines. The sound went *fft, fft, fft*, like paper leaping from a copying machine. I saw a sign, SLOW TRAFFIC AHEAD, and I made a tune for it. I sang, "She said there's slow traffic, slow traffic, slow traffic ahead." I sang about thirty variations of that, till my voice felt scratchy. I saw the sign for the state liquor store that's lit like a prison. I didn't turn in the entrance. I thought about the kindness of Roz's mouth.

AT IRVING CIRCLE K, I bought a purple can of Skoal Berry Blend and a green can of Skoal Apple Blend long-cut tobacco. At home I watched a YouTube video called "First Dip Video Skoal Cherry Longcut." A seventeen-year-old boy stuffed a mass of cherry-flavored tobacco into his cheek and spat into a jar as he talked. He'd quit smoking and now he was dipping. "One of my friends who dips says you can live without your lip but you can't live without your lungs," he said. "I support that." I watched several more first-dip videos—there are hundreds. Some of the dippers had special saliva receptacles called mud jugs. They expertly shifted enormous "hammers"—wads of wet tobacco—around in their cheeks and said "awesome" a lot. They compared flavors and brands—wintergreen versus apple, and Grizzly versus Cope, or Copenhagen. A kid named Outlawdipper filled half his face with Cope Wintergreen. "My gums have been killing me," he said. "My fricking gums are all the way receded. Maybe I should stop dipping. Nah." Talking rapidly, his personable young face deformed by the giant plug of tobacco, Outlawdipper demonstrated various styles of mud jugs available on Mudjug.com—the wood-grain mud jug, the red-bandanna mud jug, and his favorite, the carbon-fiber mud jug. "Looks gorgeous," he says. "Just messes with your mind and your eyes." A man who called himself Cutlerylover took an oversize dip. He started rubbing his temples with his fingers and said, "Ugh, I'm getting really buzzed, I definitely don't like that feeling." He turned off the camera and was gone for a while to throw up. When he came back he said, "I will never ever ever ever do that again in my entire life." I went to Mudjug.com—selling "the only spitter good enough for the Armed Forces." A sergeant in Iraq wrote a testimonial: "When we are on those long convoys, crammed inside our vehicles like sardines, there is just no where to spit without hittin' somebody," he said. But his mud jug changed all that. "I have carried this thing through some pretty rough times all through the Middle East and when the fire fights are all over, me and my Mud Jug are still there, waiting for more. It's a tough little spittoon I'll say that. God bless. Hoorah!"

I went outside and sat at the picnic table with a paper towel. It was about one a.m. After rapping smartly on the lid of the tobacco can the way you're supposed to, I sliced around the edge with my thumbnail to cut the paper seal. And then I grabbed my lower lip and made a little trough and stuffed a hairy lump of Skoal Berry Blend in there. It tasted a bit like

Skittles—like a box of Skittles found after a flood in a dirty basement. My mouth began pumping out remarkable amounts of saliva, which I spit, feeling ridiculous, on the grass. I lost control of my packed hammer—bits of tobacco began drifting around the inside of my cheeks. There was no mental effect—no rush—and then suddenly, holy mindfuckery of corned beef and cowbell, my brain converged tightly on itself and blew open. My cheekbones began singing spirituals and I laughed. There was a needly coldness in my fingers. I had a strong inclination to retch, which I mastered. Interesting how the body takes over. It seemed important all at once to spit out the brown mess and wipe off my tongue and lie down on the grass. I lay there panting for a while, saying, "God help me."

The high was extreme but short-lived. It was an unthoughtful sort of joy—too violent. No doors of perception opened. I thought of John Candy, in *Splash*, saying, "My heart's beating like a rabbit."

HOW DO YOU DO? I'm officially a resident of the United States of America. Millions of other people live in this country with me, and I don't know their names. I have lots of words in my head, bits of pop music, phrases, names of places, and scraps of poetry and prose. "Tough stuff." "Rough trade." "Party hardy." "Cheez Whiz." "Telefunken." "Matisyahu." "Znosko-Borovsky." "Misty moisty." "Serious moonlight." "Mud jug."

I have this recurring problem with my jaw that I very much want to tell you about.

But maybe not now.

No matter how hot the night, if you go out in a T-shirt and you lie on the grass for a while it's eventually going to get chilly and you're going to want shelter. That's my hard-won truth of the night. That and that Skoal Berry Blend isn't the drug for me.

Three

SOME PEOPLE I DON'T KNOW very well are coming for
tea today. I washed the dust off the teapot and found a
couple of tea bags and wiped down my grandmother's tea
tray. These semiformal social events destroy me. I spent two
hours straightening the living room and making sure the
downstairs bathroom was usable. The vacuum cleaner hose
is extremely kinked and gets clogged easily, and I had to
repair the sweeper attachment with duct tape. Why did I say
tea? Because I wanted to be welcoming and I didn't want to
give them dinner or lunch or drinks. I should have just said
come and sit in the yard and have a beer and some chips and
some green guacamole squirted from a plastic pouch—I
would be happier and probably they would be happier.

One is a poet I met in Cincinnati when I gave a reading
there last year—a woman with a friendly, loud laugh and
dramatic lipstick—and one is I think her boyfriend, who is

a filmmaker, and they want to make some kind of documentary about rhyme. Because I published an anthology, *Only Rhyme*, a few years ago, they think I can help them, perhaps with raising money or suggesting people to interview. They've got their project up on Kickstarter. And I want to say, Good luck, I can't help you very much, I'll give thirty dollars to your Kickstarter fund, but I don't know anything useful about poetry anymore. I love it, sort of, but I also don't love it and don't understand it, and every day I live, it seems more mysterious and farther away from me. But I won't say that, of course. I'll just pour the tea and hand around the plate of shortbread cookies.

HEY, JUNIOR BIRDMEN. I'm Paul Chowder and I'm here in the blindingness of noon near the chicken hut talking only to you about the things that need to be talked about. You know what they are. Love and fame and nothingness and sunken cathedrals and the Sears traveling sprinkler. Nan will be home tomorrow.

I want to be starting out. I want to be speaking in a foreign language. I want to offer an alternate route. I want to amass ragged armfuls of lucid confusion that make you keel over.

I want to write songs. Not poems anymore—songs. In fact, I made up another song in the car yesterday. It's a protest song. This is how it goes: "I'm eating a burrito, and I'm not killing anyone. / I'm eating a burrito, and I'm not killing anyone. / I'm eating a burrito, baby, and I'm not killing anyone." The tune has a little of the Who's "Behind Blue Eyes" in it.

The most useful thing I learned when I was in music school was not the augmented sixth chord, or how to write a canon at the half step, or how to scrape a certain part of the reed to make the high D easier in the bassoon solo in *The Rite of Spring*. The most useful thing I learned, I learned in orchestration class. The teacher said, "Here's the first thing you need to know: The orchestra doesn't play in tune. That's what makes it sound like an orchestra. It can't be perfectly in tune. If it was perfectly in tune, it would have an entirely different sound. It's a collective musical instrument that is always slightly out of tune with itself."

Which is also true, in a different way, of the piano. The piano is tuned to be slightly out of tune—that's part of what gives it its character. The mis-tuning is called "equal temperament." Also, wood is a complicated, tissuey substance, with columns of water in it, and sound travels from the piano wires through these long cellusonic resonators, and when it flares out into the auditorium, it's messed up slightly. It's been batted around—and now it's warmer, with a mist of imprecision over it. The timber has fogged the timbre, thereby creating the necessary out-of-tuneness, the naturalness, the untrue trueness of piano sound, or orchestral sound. That's what music relies on: the singularity of every utterance.

It turned out the Kickstarter couple weren't very interested in the shortbread cookies. They'd brought a video camera and lights, and they wanted to interview me about the history of rhyme. I said that part of what happened to rhyme in the twentieth century was that there was so much brilliant recorded lyricizing by Cole Porter, by Leiber and Stoller, by Mann and Weil, by Lennon and McCartney, and etcetera, that by the sixties and seventies the old Ella Wheeler Wilcox approach, the Sara Teasdale approach, the A. E. Housman approach, the Robert Frost approach, didn't make sense anymore, and the poets had to figure out what they could do that was artier and more elevated. And what they did was to ditch the badminton net—they ditched rhyme altogether.

As I was talking, it occurred to me that what was so appealing about song lyrics was that the music fogs over the consonants and dissolves them. "All you need is the same vowel sound and you've got a rhyme," I heard myself saying. "It's very liberating." I got my speakers and played the videomakers a song I like by Stephen Fearing, "Black Silk Gown." Stephen Fearing sings, "The night is shot with diamonds, above these dark New England towns, / And the highway drawn beneath me like a black silk gown." If it was a printed poem, the rhyme of "towns" and "gown" wouldn't sound quite right, but with the music going, it's perfect. In the studio, Fearing installs a tiny microphone inside his acoustic guitar, and the sounds he plucks from it are very big. He's a monkey-fingered madman guitar player.

After they packed up their video equipment and left, I drove to Planet Fitness and used the machines there, watching the newscasters move their mouths on the bank of television screens and listening to Donovan sing "Universal Soldier." It is a good protest song, written by Buffy Sainte-Marie. Then I got in the car and drank some Pellegrino and sweated. I sat bent over with my head on the steering wheel and let all of my self and my mind flow into my lips, so that they were swollen with unvoiced words. I thought of male actors with big lips and how if I had big lips I could stand with a slight frown and ploof out my full set of lips and maybe that would be attractive to women, since women seemed to like James Dean and other sexually ambiguous people. My lips felt like a horse's lips. Just give me an apple and I'll wimble at it. Hi, I'm Harry Connick, Jr. I would really like to be Harry Connick, Jr.

Time now to get my frequent burrito card punched again at Dos Amigos Burritos.

IT'S ALWAYS BETTER to start fresh than to rewrite. The cult of rewriting has practically sunk poetry. For instance, right now, hell, I could begin a poem with "I dusted the side table with one of her underpants." That's not a bad beginning. I could take it from there. It's true. I have an old pair of Roz's underpants, and sometimes if I have to make the living room presentable for teatime guests I squirt some Old English furniture polish on my grandmother's table, which was unfortunately refinished at one point with polyurethane, and I polish it to a nice shine.

Today I thought, My birthday is coming up, and nobody knows I want a guitar: I'll just go to Best Buy and buy myself one. So I did, admiring as I drove into the parking lot the splendid striped colors of the new sign at the Old Navy store, which is trying to relaunch itself in a changed world. Best Buy is faltering a bit, too, I'd read—nobody is buying CDs, and Netflix and other movie streamers have destroyed the DVD business, and videogame sales are off. But there was plenty of noise in the music department, and my guitar was still there. It was a Gibson Maestro. The word "Maestro" was in fifties handwriting script, and the box said: "Everything you need is right here!" I rested it on the roof of my car and tore it open. Inside was a black guitar with six strings, a black case, a strap, some picks, and a warranty. Hah, a warranty. How many of these warranty cards have I seen and thrown out in my life? A hundred? I knew the guitar would never break, and it hasn't.

I got in the car and plucked a note with my thumb on the biggest, fattest string. An almost incomprehensibly gorgeous sound gushed out of the big hole, from inside the guitar's wooden velodrome. It made something vibrate in my pituitary gland. "Ooh, that's so nice," I said.

I drove home and worked through the first few guitar

lessons in GarageBand. I practiced chords until the tips of my fingers hurt terribly. You have no idea how sharp guitar strings are. I looked at my fingers and saw deep red grooves. Fortunately the string just missed the numb skin graft on my index finger, where I once cut it slicing bread.

I wanted to play minor chords immediately, but the cheerful, well-groomed instructor from GarageBand was sitting on his stool telling me how to play major chords. They always start you off with major keys even though minor is where you generally end up.

Long years ago I wrote a poem called "Misery Hat." It was about a magical hat that the narrator, a woman, knits out of yarn from a mysterious yarn store, and when she puts it on she can sense any misery within a five-mile radius. She senses human misery and animal misery and sometimes even plant misery—the misery, for instance, of a neglected banana turning black in a bowl. She's dissatisfied with the hat and she knits a bigger one, with yellow and brown and green and black stripes, that can sense any misery anywhere in the world. She sits miserably doing nothing, wearing her long floppy hat. I sent the poem to Peter Davison, the poetry editor at *The Atlantic*. He sent it back. Later, after he'd published another poem of mine, "Knowing What to Ignore," he took me to lunch at the St. Botolph Club. I had a delicious bowl of leek soup and suddenly he leaned forward and whispered to me that Walter Cronkite was at a table across the room. I looked and, wow, there was Walter Cronkite, looking a little older than when he cried on the news after Kennedy was shot, but not that much older.

I sent Peter Davison the manuscript of my first book of poems. He'd recently published Stanley Kunitz's *The Poems of Stanley Kunitz*—a book I loved and carried around with me—and he'd bought me leek soup at the St. Botolph Club in Walter Cronkite's presence, and he'd said encouraging things, and he'd published "Knowing What to Ignore." I'd left out "Misery Hat" because I knew he didn't like it. I thought it was a good bet that he would publish my book. In the end, though, he rejected it.

But he was a genial, intelligent man—a bit of a name-dropper, perhaps, as are we all, but a nice man and a sharp-eyed editor. Oddly, the main thing I remember about him was that he wore a beautiful tie and pronounced his first name "Meter."

I LIKE WRITING in the car. I can drive somewhere, park, put my notebooks and my papers on the dashboard, clamp on my headphones, and think hard in all directions. Sometimes I put the white plastic chair in the back seat, so that I can sit beside the car when it gets too hot. The air-conditioning doesn't work anymore, and I'm always on the lookout for a place to park with dappled shade. I live for dappled shade. There's a corner of a parking lot near Planet Fitness that is particularly dappled. I thought I saw Gerard Manley Hopkins there once, in his car, muttering over a dictionary of Anglo-Saxon.

One of the small great moments in *Crazy Heart*, the movie with Jeff Bridges, comes early on, when he arrives somewhere after a long drive and the first thing he does is open his car door slightly and pour the urine from his travels onto the parking lot. It's not hard to do once you get the hang of it.

My power steering has a leak—the fluid dribbles out uncontrollably. I had it fixed once and I'm not going to fix it again until I get things settled with the IRS. So I have no power steering, and I have to struggle to maneuver into a parking space or turn a tight corner. And the brakes are getting worrisomely soft again. But it's my car, my Kia Rio, and I love it. I really love this car. No car has ever been this good to me. I will be faithful to this car forever. I will nurse it along. If, when I'm a wobbly old man wearing young man's blue jeans, the University of Texas asks me to sell them my correspondence, which they probably won't, I'll say to them, Forget the letters, forget the manuscripts, what you want is my green Kia Rio. And maybe my traveling sprinkler, too.

Four

I'M OUT IN THE GARDEN, Maud, and very fine clouds have, without my noticing, moved across the moon and collected around it like the soft gray dust in the dryer. I want to scoop the gray clouds away and see the moon naked like a white hole in the sky again, but it isn't going to happen.

About an hour ago I had a little scare. I was listening to Midnight Star playing "Freak-A-Zoid" on my headphones, that eighties standby, and I was remembering a time in music camp when a green-eyed cellist and I wrote "1976" in the sand. And then, through the music, I heard a very weird short barking sound.

What in the holy Choctaw Nation was that? I tore off my headphones. It was not a normal dog bark. Maybe a coyote bark? Not like that. Coyotes go *ooo-ooo-ooo* from miles away, mournfully. I said, "Hey there." It was quite close—it came from behind me, in the overgrown area. Did porcupines bark? No. Once at twilight I walked up to a baby porcupine near my compost bin. It screamed like a petulant child, and its mother hustled over and turned her back on me, showing her fade haircut. It sounded nothing like this. This was a definite bark. Probably the wild animal, whatever it was, had seen the glow of my computer and been frightened by it. I turned the screen to reflect its eyes, but I couldn't see any eyes.

I looked up at the moon and the squinting stars and the black masses of the trees. There was no sound except the distant chirring of crickets. I didn't want to go inside, because it was very cool outside and there were no mosquitoes and it was a perfect night for thinking, except for the unseen animal that was disconcerted by my being out here in the yard when he or she thought the world was his, or hers. I didn't want to let my dog out, because he'd smell whatever it was and go crazy barking—he's a very full-throated barker when he feels it's necessary—and wake the neighbors. Do raccoons bark? I don't think so. Somebody said they'd seen a bear near Dead Duck Beach. Do bears bark?

I heard it again, closer, still behind me. Three short loud rattling barks. Was it dying? Did it hate me? Did it care about me at all?

I was spooked. I went inside. I looked up "bark bear" on the Internet. Very little. Also "bark wolf" and "bark moose" and "bark deer." There were lots of hits for barking deer. I watched a murky YouTube video called "Barking Female Deer." The sound was exactly what I'd heard. Then YouTube wanted me to watch—and I did watch, twice—a video blooper compilation with ninety-seven million views in which a news anchorwoman mistakenly said, "Georgia is the top penis-producing state." The fallibility of newscasters was comforting. I decided to go back outside because I wasn't sleepy yet.

BACK OUTSIDE, I looked around and noticed that Nan's kitchen light was on. Then I saw her. She was in her bathrobe, walking slowly back from the chicken hut. Her hair was undone. She usually wore it up.

I went over. "Nan?" I called.

"Hi," she said.

"Did you hear that?"

"The barking deer?"

I nodded. "It totally freaked me out. It was right behind me."

"Yeah, I heard it about a month ago, too."

I sensed something in her voice and asked her what was wrong. I figured it might be trouble with Chuck.

"Oh, my mom's not doing well. She was allergic to the painkiller and she got something called Emergency Room Psychosis, and she was having delusions, and now she's got pneumonia on top of that. It's just endless."

"Oh, gosh, I'm so sorry," I said.

"Chuck's away consulting in Korea, which is frustrating. And Raymond's been in Boston a lot visiting his girlfriend. I miss having him around."

"Of course," I said. Raymond is Nan's son, a tall amiable long-haired young man of about nineteen who's into music. Nan invited me to his high school graduation, but I couldn't go because I was giving a reading at U Penn.

I thought maybe I should hug Nan, but I didn't because it was late at night and she was wearing a bathrobe. I said, "I'm right here, as you know." I gestured toward the henhouse. "I can easily do the chickens."

"Thanks, I really like doing the chickens, but yes, if I have to go back to Toronto, I'd appreciate some help. I'm sorry to lay this on you. Nice moon."

"Very nice moon," I said. "Also, I was thinking I could water your tomatoes with my traveling sprinkler. If it would help in any way."

"That's very kind of you, but Raymond should be coming back tomorrow," she said. "I guess I should go in. Nice to see you. You're up late."

"I like looking at the sky," I said.

"Me, too." Then she reconsidered. "Actually, there is something you could do that would be very helpful."

"Sure, what?"

She said that Raymond had been working like a fiend on some songs and he seemed happy about them and he'd been writing the lyrics in a little notebook, but he didn't want to play them for her because they were inappropriate. "I guess they're hip-hop or something," she said. "He likes the fact that you're a poet, and I think he'd like you to hear them. Or I'd like you to hear them."

I said sure, I'd love to hear his songs. "I'm no expert on Biggie Smalls, but I just got a guitar and it would be fun to hear what he's been up to." Then suddenly I had a thought. "Why don't you and Raymond come over sometime and we can have dinner and then he can play me his songs and you can put your fingers in your ears. I could get takeout sushi."

"That's a nice idea," she said. "Raymond loves California roll."

"Great," I said. So Nan and Raymond are coming to dinner. Fortunately the downstairs bathroom's still clean from the video couple's visit. I've got to get some songs together to play for them. Casually available for singing, if it comes to that. I've got to be able to hold my head up.

I'M OUT IN MY KIA RIO with the door open at eleven in the morning, the day after the barking deer episode. Get back on the horse. Today there is only one agitated bird. A nice thing happened to me last night—Nan asked me for help. I feel honored. I wish there was something I could do to help her, or her mother. All politics is local. I wish I could write Nan a song. I gave it a try, using some of the chords I've learned, an A minor chord and a D minor chord and a seventh chord. The chorus was: "I wish there was something I could do for you."

My fingertips are profoundly numb from too much guitar. They feel like little white islands.

HEY HEY HEY. Let me try to get it together. Deep breath now. Hide the things that you're most embarrassed by. Nobody's going to care, but hide them anyway. I have so much in my head that's screaming to get out. Politely requesting passage. Sometimes knowing things and knowing that you'll never unknow them, unless you say them, is really unbearable.

Here's my Traveling Sprinkler file. It's fat with patent records that I've printed out from the patent office. Some people call them walking sprinklers. I talked to a man in North Platte, Nebraska, named Ed Saulsbury, who restored traveling sprinklers. Back before I got distracted by the wars in Afghanistan and Iraq, I was going to write a poem about Ed, and I bought two very interesting vintage sprinklers on eBay. I wrote part of the poem and then I put it away, and then a few months ago, I thought I'd call Ed and see how he was doing, and it turned out that he'd died in 2007. He'd been a utility pole climber, servicing power lines.

In *New and Selected Poems, Volume Two*, Mary Oliver has a prose poem about a black jet flying over a hummingbird. "All narrative is metaphor," she says. Or is it "All metaphor is narrative"?

I GOT OUT OF THE SHOWER this morning and didn't want to go to Planet Fitness, so I put a pillow under my bottom and hooked my feet under the bed and did some sit-ups while reading a poem by Léonie Adams. There's a scene in one of John Wayne's last movies, where he's puffy-faced and sick from cancer, which he got either from playing Genghis Khan in a radioactive valley downwind of the Yucca Flat nuclear test site, or from smoking four packs of Camels a day. In the movie, Wayne dies in a big shoot-out, with Opie of *The Andy Griffith Show* looking on sadly, but before he dies he rides for a long time on a horse-drawn streetcar. He has a talk with a fresh-faced young woman and remembers his love for Lauren Bacall. Then, just as he's about to disembark from the streetcar, he gives the conductor a fancy whorehouse pillow that he's been carrying around with him. "These old bones surely thank you," says the conductor, sitting on the pillow.

I thought of John Wayne's red pillow as I did my sit-ups and read Léonie Adams. I got to the second-to-last line of the poem: "My every leaf leans forth upon the day." Good line. Adams was influenced by the Elizabethan songsters. She wanted to sing densely, like Campion and Dowland. She taught at Bennington and had a brief affair with Edmund Wilson. Wilson, who was married, got her pregnant, and she had a miscarriage and grieved over it. He was such a low, mean, drunken bug of a critic. He jeered at Tolkien's *Lord of the Rings* and wrote a vicious but accurate parody of Archibald MacLeish for *The New Yorker* called "The Omelet of A. MacLeish." MacLeish was never the same after Edmund Wilson's parody. He began writing urgent bad speeches in favor of intervention in the Spanish Civil War, and then Roosevelt asked him to be Librarian of Congress.

I've been reading about protest songs on the Internet. Somebody recommended one called "Living Darfur."

BEST BUY GIVES YOU one free lesson if you buy a guitar, so I signed up with a man who teaches progressive rock. When I think of beginning lessons again, though, it really hurts. All those years of bassoon lessons I took. All those Milde études I learned. All those years of soaking my reed in a baby food jar and croaking it to see that it was still healthy and hearing the tick tock of my red plastic Taktell metronome perched on the edge of the piano. My teacher, Bill Brown, was a student of Norman Herzberg, the great studio bassoonist in Los Angeles. You can hear Herzberg's bassoon in *E.T.*, in *Jaws*, in Bugs Bunny and Road Runner cartoons, and in the theme music to *The Alfred Hitchcock Hour*. Herzberg was a Zen Buddhist of bassoon, and Billy Brown taught me his method of meditating while practicing. The meditation was called "long tones."

A long tone was a note that you played for sixteen beats of the Super-Mini-Taktell metronome. You started as softly as you could, at *pppppp*, the way you would start the low E in Tchaikovsky's *Symphonie Pathétique*, and you held that for four beats and then you did a very slow and very perfectly graduated increase in sound, letting just the right amount of air into the reed and never varying the pitch and never adding any falsification of vibrato, and eventually you were playing as loudly as you could and yet with perfect control, for four more beats, squandering all your lung air, but you still had to keep steady and do a perfect diminuendo for four beats and go all the way back down to an extreme pianissimo for four beats. One day you'd do long tones on a low E and the next maybe you'd concentrate on a middle A flat, and you would do this for every note in the full range of the instrument. This was discipline. And while you did it you emptied your mind of everything except that note—which you were hoping would become, would truly achieve, the fully rounded bassoonistic sort of note that you'd heard the great virtuosi play, men like Herzberg, or Bernie Garfield in Philadelphia, or Maurice Allard in Paris, or Simon Kovar, wherever he was. Simon Kovar had edited a number of practice books for the bassoon, including the Milde études and the Pierné études, and he'd recorded a performance of Mozart's bassoon concerto. He was one of our minor deities. Gabriel Pierné was a conservatory friend of Debussy's and a sometime conductor. He conducted the first performance of Stravinsky's *Firebird*, which has a brain-melting bassoon lullaby in it.

Debussy liked the bassoon a lot, although not quite as much as Stravinsky. Debussy once judged a woodwind competition at the conservatoire. He'd been feeling very low, he wrote to a young composer, feeling as if he'd prefer to be a sponge at the bottom of the sea or a vase on the mantelpiece, "anything rather than a man of intellect." This was in 1909, a year before he finished his tenth piano prelude, "The Sunken Cathedral." But the student woodwind players cheered him up mightily. The bassoonists were assigned a fantasy by Henri Büsser, a piece written, Debussy said, as if Büsser had been born in a bassoon—"which is not to say he was born to make music." The bassoons, according to Debussy, were as *pathétique* as Tchaikovsky and as ironic as Jules Renard. And then Debussy judged a piano competition. The best player was a thirteen-year-old Brazilian girl whose eyes were, he said, "drunk with music." Debussy's own daughter, whom they called Chouchou, was a genius of a girl of twelve when her father died in 1918, with the sound of the long-range German guns booming outside Paris. "I saw him one last time in that horrible box," she wrote to her stepbrother. "Tears restrained are worth as much as tears shed, and now it is night for ever. Papa is dead." A year later she died, of diphtheria and medical malpractice.

After Debussy died, Henri Büsser, born in a bassoon, orchestrated "The Sunken Cathedral," kitsching up the score with harp glissandi. It was a hopeless thing for Büsser to try to do, because the real sunken cathedral was Debussy's own Blüthner grand piano, with its ineffably soft tone. He liked to play it with the top down.

Five

HELLO AND WELCOME to the Paul Chowder Hour. I'm your host, and I hope by this time that I'm your friend, and I want you to know something. When you have me as a friend, you have somebody you can count on. If you need help, I'll be there. Like if you need me to help you dig in some bulbs, or water your tomatoes, or carry your groceries, or tend your chickens, I can do that. The only thing I can't do is I can't call you up and be hearty and affectionate and cheerful if you're mortally ill. That I can't do. I've done it several times, but I don't do a good job of it, because when I know somebody's dying it's just so sad and awful that I can't pretend that it's not.

Today we've got a couple of important things to talk about. I woke up at one-thirty this morning and I thought, This is the perfect time: one-thirty in the morning. Is there a better time of day or night to explain whatever seems to need explaining? No. It's all there in that time: one-thirty. Half past one. It's not that late. Lots of people are up at one-thirty. It's not insomnia. It's not early rising. It's just that you're up at one-thirty. I bet Bach was often up at one-thirty arpeggiating away at his freshly tuned harpsichord.

I went outside and sat in the green metal chair and tried to further my understanding of the problem of metaphorical interference. It's a serious problem, at least for me. What is metaphorical interference? Okay, well, it's when two or more strong metaphors are podcasting in the same room together and they mess with each other. They mix, but not necessarily in the very same sentence the way a classic mixed metaphor mixes. They mix structurally. Say, for example, that you've decided to mention the traveling sprinkler in your poem. The moment you mention it, it starts to twirl and hiss and spray water everywhere. It becomes a controlling metaphor. There's no help for it, you're going to get wet.

But then say the traveling sprinkler seems to be tightly connected in your mind, perhaps by a long, pale green hose, to another idea that interests you, which is Debussy's piano prelude "The Sunken Cathedral." You think you're still all right, because one is a real object and the other is a piece of classical music that contains a metaphor of submergence. But then you remember that some yellowjackets have made their nest in the hollow plastic handle of the hose reel. This happens to me every summer. I know that if Nan says that I can set up the sprinkler's hose route around her tomatoes, I'm going to need my hose as well as her hose, and I know that as soon as I start wheeling the hose reel around and pulling the hose off it the yellowjackets are going to fly out and dart at me angrily and sting me as I run away. I don't want to be stung, so I'll debate whether I should boil up a pasta pot of water and pour it on the hose-reel handle, destroying the yellowjacket nest. My friend Tim told me about this technique, and I did it two summers ago before my sister and her family came for lunch at the picnic table, and it definitely worked, but I felt horrible afterward. What right did I have to destroy a whole happy nest of insects, regardless of how annoying they are when they crawl around on the potato chips?

Now your poem is in trouble. You've got wasps in the hose reel, you've got the sprinkler twirling at the end of the hose, and you've got Debussy's cathedral sunk under the waves. You've got fish, you've got tomatoes. You're starting to get strange purple interference patterns, fringe moiré patterns, at the edges of each metaphor, where it overlaps its neighbor. Photographers call this "purple fringing," and it's a flaw. This is the moment when your creative writing teacher may say: "You've got an awful lot going on here, Paul. Maybe you need to pare this poem down and pick a controlling image."

And you acknowledge that he has a point—too many colors make the rinse water muddy. We know that. On the other hand, the world is full of metaphors that are happily coexisting in our brains and we don't go crazy. You have them all swarming and nesting and reeled up in there, but they don't trouble one another. One moment you entertain one metaphor, and the next moment the next, no harm done. And this time you think, I don't want to worry so much about this rhetorical non-problem. I want to pour them all in and let them go wild together. Let all the metaphors fuck each other like desperate spouse-swappers, I don't care. I summarily reject this notion of metaphorical interference for the time being and I'm putting it aside and I'm going to think over the things that call forth thought, and if they get in one another's way from time to time that's just what happens. It's my poem. I don't care what Peter Davison might think. He's gone now and God rest him.

I WANT TO REALLY BE with a woman. By that I mean I want to be able to stay up late with her talking about everything. I want to show her all the things that I've found out, which aren't very interesting maybe, but they're what I have. And I want her to show me all the things that she's found out.

I'd rather not spend two hours a day reading political blogs, or flipping through *People* magazine at the supermarket checkout, or watching old episodes of *The Office*. What good does it do me to read Glenn Greenwald's excellent blog? He's right about everything and I'm glad he's doing it, but it doesn't seem to have any effect.

I want to confide—that's what I want to do. What confiding is is that you have a woman you like a great deal and you tell her things that you didn't even know were secrets. You look at her and you feel a nervous warmth because she's the only person who will understand. She's just said something so direct and so interesting—something you never heard before—and suddenly all of the distractions of people's opinions swirling around you stop. You hear just this one woman next to you saying this one opinion that's coming out of her mouth, and you think, I could listen to her say things forever.

Roz and I are—I don't want to say we're finished, because we're really not. We're still good friends and we talk on the phone and I sometimes send her postcards when I'm lonely in hotel rooms. I still hold out hope. She's promised to make me an egg salad sandwich on my birthday, after all. But it doesn't look good. She's very busy with her radio show. She produces a medical radio show called *Medicine Ball* in the expensive new NPR building in Concord, where everything is carpeted and hushed and all the microphones are state-of-the-art, even if monophonic. It's a successful show, it's syndicated, it's good. Every week they discuss the side effects and potential harmful outcomes of at least one pill or medical procedure. They did an extremely good show on Lipitor. Who knew that Lipitor could be so interesting? A totally useless drug, it seems. You take it for years and it makes you dizzy and forgetful and you fall down and break your hip.

Roz has taken up with this very articulate doctor from Dartmouth who has strong contrary opinions about the medical establishment. He's a doctor who reads—not just research papers on Lipitor, but books. He fancies himself a sort of Oliver Sacks, I think. Last time I talked to her she said they were reading Tony Hoagland's poetry together. What a horrible thing to imagine. I like Tony Hoagland's poetry. I want to be reading it with her. The doctor has a low, growly radio voice. Apparently he "makes her laugh." I know that kind of laughter. Sexual laughter.

MY BASSOON WAS a Heckel bassoon, made of maplewood, stained very dark, almost black, with a nickel-plated ring on top. I loved it because it looked like a strange undersea plant, something that would live in the darkness of the Marianas Trench, near a toxic fumarole. My wonderful grandparents bought it for me, and I performed Rimsky-Korsakov's *Scheherazade* on it, and Ravel's *Bolero*, and Stravinsky's *Firebird Suite*, and Vivaldi's A minor bassoon concerto. I put in thousands of hours of practice, shredding my lips, permanently pushing my two front teeth apart. And then I decided I wasn't going to be a musician, because I wasn't that good, and my jaw was hurting badly and I had headaches from too much blowing. I was going to be a poet instead. I sold my beloved Heckel to Bill, my bassoon teacher, for ten thousand dollars. Suddenly I felt free and very rich. I quit music school and flew to Berkeley, California, and took a poetry class with Robert Hass, who was a good teacher.

In Berkeley I heard Robert Hass read his somewhat famous and presumably autobiographical poem about an almost affair he'd had with an Asian woman who'd had a double mastectomy. She leaves a bowl of dead bees outside his door. It's quite a poem when read aloud.

BACK LAST FALL, when I wasn't writing much of anything—not because I was "blocked," but because what I wrote wasn't any good—I signed up for Match.com and I answered the questionnaire and I went out on a date. It didn't feel like a date, exactly, because a date is such a fifties notion, but it was a date. In other words, I was out wearing a corduroy jacket one evening, sitting in a restaurant with a folksinger named Polly. Paul and Polly.

That's all I'll tell you about it. I was sitting at the same table with Polly, near the fireplace, over which hung an enormous blue-green fish. That's all you need to know. She was my "date." You don't need to know anything more about her. We were not in any sense together, nothing like that— that beautiful word, "together." We were talking about Marvin Gaye's tragic death and cider doughnuts and how amazing it is that we can both speak English. We were describing all the things we had to know in order to speak this crazy messed-up language.

There was a little round moderno light above our table, sending down rays of electric energy onto our salads, and I could see the lightbulb reflected in Polly's lipstick, and suddenly I told her that I was so happy to be sitting at the table with her that I wanted to get up and embrace the light and say thank you for lighting up our dinner. Because we are enjoying ourselves, and we're covering a lot of ground, and we're ranging wide over the field of human aspirations, and this is what we've got right now, is this single date in a restaurant.

I wanted to say more to Polly because I knew it was going well, even though she didn't like me as much as I liked her, and I knew that was because she was smarter and more sensible and mainly prettier than I was smart or sensible or good-looking. I said, "Polly, let me ask you this. Do you think all of our selves are pointed at this moment right here in this restaurant?" I tapped the bread in the breadbasket. It was a basket of bread, tucked in with a white cloth like a newborn child. I said, "Do you think that the bread in this breadbasket is the only thing in life right now?"

She said, "In a way I do. But in a way I think of the whole city stretched out, and of other cities, and of distances between cities, and of long train rides or plane rides to get from one city to another, so I try to keep mindful of the fact that my moment isn't the entire moment, but it's difficult especially when I'm having fun and when I'm talking to a nice man in a restaurant."

Wow, I felt a glow when she said that. Then a little later she said how much she liked Philip Glass's movie soundtracks. Well, all right, I thought, with some effort I can learn to like Philip Glass's soundtracks. They're insanely repetitive, but I can come around. Then I made a dumb move. We were on the topic of Mark Rothko, and for some inexplicable reason I was moved to say critical things not only about Mark Rothko but also about Pablo Picasso. Why, why, why? I said Picasso would be all but forgotten in a hundred years, that he was a coattail-rider and a self-trumpeter, and that his kitschy blue guitars made me want to scream with boredom and rage at the moneyed injustice of the international museum establishment. And that those awful demoiselles from Avignon were nothing but a hideous cruel joke. And that he consistently ripped off Matisse. And not only that, but his daughter's jewelry designs for Tiffany's were just god-awful. There were, I said, innumerable Sunday painters who could paint better than shirtless old Pablo—and at some point we'd have to face that stark, appalling fact. I could see Polly flinch. I quickly apologized for being stupidly opinionated and said that I didn't know anything about art and that actually I liked Picasso's flashlight painting and his steer's head made of bicycle parts, although Duchamp, et cetera, and we got back on track. Later she said, "I'm having fun." But I knew she was just being nice because the wine was red and she was so very pretty and such a kindly person and she didn't want me to know that she was never going to go out with me again because I'm a rogue mastodon who dismisses Picasso with an annoying wave of his trunk. She wanted me to think that the world is a place in which somebody like me could go out with somebody like her. She wanted me to think that she was a person who didn't become infatuated with bad standoffish married men who dressed in leather car coats. But it turned out she was.

I COULD SEE the dismissal in the corners of Polly's eyes. I could see that she was interested in talking to me, interested in knowing an anthologist of minor notoriety, and maybe in being my friend, all that junk—but that she probably wasn't going to be my girlfriend. And that's the thing I wanted. I wanted that little jingly bell in front of the word "friend": girlfriend. I'm a boy—a boy in his mid-fifties—and here is my friend, who is a girl. I wanted to have her next to me when we were walking and to be able to put my arm around her shoulder and draw her to me so that she stumbled a bit, happily, smiling at her stumbling. This was not in the cards.

No book review section can help you with this. No movie, no blog, no self-help book. Nothing helps, because it's all new. It's something two people make up as they go along. I called her up again and told her there was an Indian place I knew where they made memorable fried eggplant balls. Then she laid the truth on me. She told me that she had something going with a somewhat famous literary man, a married man who lived in New York, and it was turning into a terrible ordeal because he probably wasn't ever going to leave his marriage, but there it was and she couldn't escape her feelings, she had to live through them. She even told me who the man was. I looked up some pictures of him. I won't tell you his name. But there he was in a photograph with his secretive successful smile, wearing a leather car coat. And that was that.

Boy, she was pretty, though. I waggled my Shropshire lad that night.

Six

I'M SITTING in a very small park in Portsmouth, New Hampshire, where I live. There are two branches that face each other across a square of mulch and a weeping fruit tree in the middle. I have a corncob pipe between my middle molars. It has a yellow plastic stem and it was made in Missouri. The tobacco came from Turkey—it was a special kind of tobacco, said the tobacconist at Federal Cigar, who was apportioning it into plastic bags with zip tops. The reason it's so special is that it was dried over a smoky fire. In other words, it's smoked tobacco that you smoke. One bag cost eight dollars, and the corncob pipe cost five dollars. The only thing I don't like about the pipe is that I can taste the yellow plastic of the stem, which has a flavor of Bic pens, and if I'm going to be chewing on something I'd rather be chewing on wood. The smoke itself seems to be turning my tongue into a pink tranche of smoked salmon.

There's a protest outside the North Church today—high school kids with a big sign that says "Occupy," and what they're protesting is global warming. What a hopeless cause. The earth has been warming and cooling for a billion years and they want it to stop. Why not protest actions that we can easily end, like the intentional killing of people with missiles in foreign countries? Start small.

One thing that interests me is how long it takes to smoke a pipe. I'm stoned out of my brain stem right now, and there still seems to be a lot of smoked turkey left in the cob. Fortunately there's a strong sideways wind.

THIS MORNING I read some articles on how to get better posture. The best advice I found was to imagine your nipples and then imagine your way four inches down on your rib cage below them and then imagine that two large steel hooks had hooked under two ribs and were pulling you diagonally up toward the sky. When you do this you immediately sit with better posture. And you really have to imagine your own nipples only once, thank God.

I want to improve myself in a dozen ways. But my fingers are trembling because of the pipe tobacco and I feel a little queasy.

I should be standing outside one of President Obama's campaign offices with a sign that says "Our President Is Killing People." The next day my sign would be: "Abolish the CIA." And the next day the sign would be: "Drones

Are Bad News for Civilization." My friend Tim goes to marches and carries signs, and he says it feels good. He got arrested once.

A bird has dropped a half-eaten berry on my keyboard. It landed on the tilde key. Maybe it was not half eaten but fully shat. I put my corncob pipe down and blew on the dark fragment of berry and it hopped away onto the mulch next to the metal bench. I imagined the two hooks winching me up, lifting my slouching corpse skyward.

A man walked past, smoking a cigarette, wearing a black stoner T-shirt. "How are you doing?" I said, waving my new pipe at him. "Not bad, and you?" He walked away across the parking lot.

TODAY IS A CLOUDY DAY. I woke up and I was amazed by how completely roasted and smoked my tongue felt. It's been many hours since I smoked a pipe, and my tongue is still recovering. It was a piece of meat in my mouth that didn't want to be steak or corned beef, it wanted still to be my own tongue. My very own talker, my slipper and slapper of mysteries.

I could be on the elliptical trainer at Planet Fitness listening to pumping music right now. The slogan of Planet Fitness is that it's the "Judgment Free Zone." You can be fat or thin, old or young, and they want you there exercising. I try to go every other, every third, day.

The problem with the corncob pipe, aside from the fact

that it bothers my jaw and roasts my tongue, is that I feel as if I'm impersonating Vannevar Bush. Bush was a famous war scientist who helped create the atomic bomb, and he also was a great pipe smoker and a great carver of pipes. He made presents of his handmade pipes to his cold-warrior friends. He gave a pipe to James Conant, the head of Harvard University and purger of Communists, and he gave a pipe to Allen Dulles, head of the CIA. "I trust," Bush wrote to Dulles, "that the pressure of the administration will not be so intense that you cannot find the time occasionally to put your feet on the desk, smoke the old pipe, and puzzle out the course of affairs in the queer world we live in."

Dulles replied on CIA letterhead—an eagle poised on a shield bearing a strange crystal star. "As I write these lines I am smoking with contentment, and no little pride, the pipe which bears your initials and which I know is your own handiwork," he said.

Perhaps Allen Dulles smoked Vannevar Bush's pipe as he mulled over the CIA's coup in Iran and the assassination of Patrice Lumumba in the Congo.

Seven

I ALMOST SKIPPED QUAKER MEETING because I hadn't
had a shower and it's hard to sit silently for an hour if
you're not clean, but then I went anyway. As I drove I listened
to Beth Orton sing a song that goes: "I don't want to know
about evil, only want to know about love." I think that's very
true. Sometimes you don't want to know about evil, you just
want to know about love. You want to take off the misery hat
and think only about the good things.

When I got inside, the clock was ticking and I was two
minutes late and discombobulated, and it took me a while to
settle down. I held my car keys. I always hold my keys during
meeting. I clutch them at first and later my grip relaxes and I
feel the smooth mountain range with my thumb.

Excuse me now while I throat-clear. Harrooom! God,
that's nasty. As soon as I start talking into this thing—this
little Olympus recorder—my vocal cords become coated

with a resistant substance that has to be ground away by an enormous throat process. And then it's as if I'm a kid who's fallen on his bicycle and skinned his knee: there's this damaged, wrecked, injured vocal cord, with half of its phlegm scraped away and half still there. It's just really revolting. I'm sorry about it. It's a product of my own nervousness. I have to overcome some powerful desire to be entirely private by talking to myself in this almost public way. Whisper-talking. Breaking the silence.

THE IDEA OF BREAKING THE SILENCE is important in Quakerism. You don't want to break it. You want to wait for it to stop being brittle. You want to ease into it, merge with it, and find that you are speaking. I think I'm becoming a Quaker, even though I don't believe in God. "God" is an embarrassing word. I can't say it without getting a strange, hollow, do-gooderish feeling in my throat. Gourd. Gawd. Gaudí. Mentally I substitute the word "good" for "God," and that helps. Good is God.

I started going to Kittery Friends Meeting a few years ago. My friend Tim had a very nice, very smart girlfriend, Hannah, who was a Quaker, and she'd gotten him going to meeting with her, and one day he was explaining to me how great it was and how there were some quite nice seemingly unattached women there who went almost every Sunday and I remembered that John Greenleaf Whittier was a Quaker and I thought, Why not go and see? I thought I wasn't going to speak, but gradually the silence got to me. A half hour passed, and then forty minutes, and someone said something about two stones side by side in a river and my blood started pounding in my ears and with five minutes to go until meeting ended I stood and said something cryptic about the incredible uncertainty of joy. I sat down shaking, trembling, quaking.

I went back two weeks later. Hannah broke up with Tim and moved away, and Tim got a better job at Tufts University, but I've been an attender at Kittery Friends Meeting on and off since. That's what you are: you're an attender. After you're an attender for a while, you can become a member, but I'm happy just being an attender.

I HAVEN'T MOWED the lawn recently because I don't want to buzz through all the dandelions. My new plan is to smoke one enormous ugly cigar per week. Just one—or two, or three, or twelve if it's necessary. A huge nasty grotesque cigar, not from Cuba, because fifty years ago Kennedy imposed a trade embargo on cigars—first securing twelve hundred H. Upmann Petit Coronas for himself and his friends—and since then we have tortured and isolated that impoverished country, all because its inhabitants "embraced" Communism. What they embraced is a hope that things could be better. That's all they embraced. These tags that people use: freedom fighter, terrorist, Communist, fellow traveler, dupe, stooge. I want to forgive everyone. I want to do better with my life. Maybe doing better is somehow finding a way to make people's imaginations work better.

Imagine a drone. Can you imagine a drone? An unmanned aerial killing machine? I will try. I read that they sound like lawnmowers. Here I am in my driveway, listening, and— yes—I can hear a distant lawnmower. What if I knew that that aerial lawnmower could at any moment blow up my house? What if in trying to blow up my house it blew up Nan's house, killing the chickens, killing both her and Raymond?

Tim told me he's going to write a book about drones. A few years ago he went to the Hannah Arendt conference at Bard College, where a man from Atlanta gave a talk on robot warfare and how it was inevitable, and how very soon drones would have software that incorporated the rules of warfare so that onboard drone computers could decide, using either-or algorithms, whether a target was legitimate and whether a missile attack would result in an acceptably low number of civilian casualties. Then the drones would not need any human operators living in Syracuse or Nevada. No human person would ever have to push a button to fire a drone missile. Everything would be preprogrammed and hands-free and guilt-free. Tim came back from the Bard conference very upset, and he began making notes for his drone meditation. Will Tim's book do anything at all to stop targeted killing? Possibly. Probably not. I have no faith in books to stop anything. You need something more than a book. If I wrote a poem against drones, would that help? Not a chance. You need more than words. You need shouting. You need crowds of people sitting down in the road. You need audible outrage.

I have just reread parts of the article in *The New York Times* that upset me so much. It's about President Obama's kill list. Why is a kill list a bad thing?

It's a bad thing because—oh gosh, where to begin.

I BOUGHT SOME BUNNY-LUV CARROTS and a bottle of Pellegrino and I aired out the picnic basket in the sun so that it would smell fresh. Then I remembered my car. It was a horrendous mess—papers were in there, and paperbacks, bags of old things, empty pouches of Planter's trail mix ("Join Mr. Peanut on a taste adventure"), sand, and now cigar ash. The ashtray was positively Pompeiian. It wasn't up to birthday snuff. I drove to the convenience store and I threw out all the trash and put quarters in the jukebox of emptiness and vacuumed the sand out of the passenger side—and the old ends of antacid, and the very dirty pennies that were stuck together from coffee spills. I heard the coins clack up the hose and I liked the sound, and I heard the sand granulate up the hose and I liked that sound, too. But still the car wasn't clean.

I went to the gas pump and got some paper towels and I dipped them into the squeegee water and cleaned the mud and dirt off the edges of the passenger door. That's the first thing you see when you open the door. I got the car looking reasonably kempt, as if I wasn't some homeless guy with a decrepit car. While I was cleaning, the smell of the windshield water got to me and I started to think, You sad fool, you're preparing for this picnic as if it's a date, but it's not. You're seeing your dear friend Roz. You're not winning her back.

I WANT TO KNOW more about songwriters. I went to Antiquarian Books on Lafayette Road to look through the music shelves. John, the owner, who is an enthusiastic member of Mensa, says he has a quarter of a million books, plus a Babylonian tablet in storage that he wants to sell for one point five million dollars. His aisles are ten feet high and double-stacked on each side with book piles—some of the aisles are so completely booked in and narrow that you have to walk sideways. John has gotten a bit portly, and some aisles he hasn't been able to fit into for years. He has an adults-only collection in the back—I've bought some racy things there to read with Roz.

This time I bought Chuck Berry's memoirs, a biography of Kurt Cobain, and a scarce collection called *Outstanding Song-Poems and Lyricists*, edited by a theatrical agent, which has many hundreds of songs written by obscure men and women who, in 1941, were eagerly hoping for their words to be set to music. There were love poems and antiwar poems and pro-war poems, all waiting for singers to sing them. On page 206, I read the beginning of a song by Mrs. Percy Halbach:

The nights were new; what did you do?
You ruined my life completely; we were making love so
   sweetly
You big bad moon.

Not too shabby, Mrs. Halbach. John said, "My best customers are the submarine men, because they never get claustrophobia when they're halfway down an aisle." When I left, John was negotiating with a cheerful couple who wanted cash for their trunkful of nineties VHS porno tapes.

I parked in the Starbucks parking lot and lit a Murciélago cigar with a black bat on the label—*murciélago* means "bat" in Spanish—and began reading about heroin overdosages in Kurt Cobain's biography. Suddenly there was a crunch and the car lurched forward. My head was thrown back and my new Craftsman's Bench cigar cutter flew into my coffee. I said, "What the fuck?" and got out, expecting to see damaged metal. A young woman with hoop earrings emerged from a big white sedan, her hand on her clavicle. She'd backed right into me. "I am so, so, so sorry," she said. We studied our bumpers—no harm done. She apologized again. I said, "I've done it myself, it's all good, no worries, bye." She got in her car and drove off. A lot of life is like that.

IT'S AMAZING TO SEE the little kids in Quaker meeting, how they learn to sit quietly. They only have to sit for fifteen minutes, and then they go downstairs to paint peace signs on stones, but at first they can't do it and they poke each other and laugh and twist in the pews and climb on their parents' laps and whisper and tap their feet. Or they page through picture books. You can hear the long, slow turning of their wider-than-it-is-tall books. It's like the pages are being cut with a paper cutter, schwooof. Then eventually the silence begins to work on them. There's a Swiss writer who wrote a book called *God Is Silence*.

The dumbest thing I ever did was not having children. Absolute dumbest thing. Even worse than selling my bassoon. I see the error now. My sister's kids are turning out great. They were shockingly spoiled when they were little, but now their true personalities have taken over and they're just nice calm tall young people with personalities. One is at Kenyon College studying something with lasers and the other is an intern at a dollhouse museum.

Nan's son Raymond is another great kid. He has gotten deeply into music in the last few years. Nan seems to think that I might serve as a role model for him, which is completely wrong but flattering. He refused to do homework and he didn't want to go to college, and instead he's in his room making beats on a beat-making machine with square rubber pads. In the summer he works at Seacoast Nursery hauling around baby trees, and he spends his money on music equipment. A few years ago I heard him banging away on a drum set. Gradually he got better. He had a good rhythmic ear. Then I heard him playing the electric guitar—that was last year. Now I don't hear him because he works with headphones on.

He reminds me a little of me in his single-mindedness, except that he's doing pop music and I was doing classical music in high school. I barely passed Algebra II and I refused to write papers on *King Lear*, which I thought was an unbearable, false, vile jelly of a play with no beauty in it anywhere, and instead I read Aaron Copland's book on music and Rimsky-Korsakov on orchestration. Rimsky-Korsakov really understood the bassoon—that's why he gave it *Scheherazade*'s D minor solo. In minor keys, Rimsky-Korsakov wrote, the bassoon has a "sad, ailing quality," while in major keys it creates an "atmosphere of senile mockery."

I read some of Stravinsky's books, too, all written with the help of the overly allusive Robert Craft, including the one where he says, "I am the vessel through which *Le Sacre* passed." And I read one of Paul Hindemith's books. Hindemith, a composer, outraged me when he wrote that the bassoon, "with its clattering long levers and other obsolete features left in a somewhat fossil condition," was due for a major overhaul. I had to admit, though, that the keys did make a lot of noise. There's no way to play a fast passage without some extraneous clacking. Listen to *Scheherazade*— you'll hear all kinds of precise metallic noises coming from the bassoonist.

I secretly wanted to be a composer, and when I wasn't practicing bassoon I was at our old Chickering piano, plinking away, writing scraps of piano sonatas in a little stave-lined notebook that I still have. And then I read Keats's sonnet and realized I wasn't going to have any success as a composer. I went to Berkeley for a while, and then to France, where I discovered Rimbaud's *Illuminations*—Rimbaud is a great sea poet—and while I was in Paris some Smith College students gave a party and I danced with two smiley girls, one in a skirt and one in sexy plaid pants, and I discovered that I enjoyed dancing with smiley Smith girls. When I got home to America, *Saturday Night Fever* was playing in movie theaters, and Elvis Costello was watching the detectives, and the Talking Heads were doing "Take Me to the River," and I suddenly thought, I've missed the boat, I want to hear music I can dance to.

Eight

I'M IN THE PARKING LOT of Margarita's, which is one strip mall over from Planet Fitness. I've been listening to a good songwriting podcast from England called *Sodajerker* while watching the latest developments in the Kardashian family saga on one of the Planet Fitness TVs. Barry Mann and Cynthia Weil, the married couple who wrote "We Gotta Get Out of This Place" for the Animals, and many other hits, told the *Sodajerker* podcasters about how they sometimes wrote "slump songs" together—songs written just so they were writing something. And some of the slump songs became hits.

"You're going to have to face it," says Robert Palmer, "you're addicted to love." I'm debating whether I should go into Margarita's and have dinner at the bar. You can order what's called a Mexican Flag, which is three different enchiladas. I think I won't, because when you eat at the bar you can't read.

Here's what happened at Quaker meeting. I listened to the clock, as I always do. Very few people spoke. A man I didn't know stood almost at the end of meeting and said his wife had died. He was quite an old man, with strong cheekbones, thin, and he held his hands out for a moment before he spoke. He said, "My wife died in my arms last week. I was lucky enough to know her for almost ten years. We met in a drawing class and I remember being impressed by how intensely she concentrated while she was drawing. She drew a pear. We were all drawing pears, but her pear made sense. It sat on the plate. I told her how much I liked her drawing, and we became friends and it turned out we were both ready to love and we got married very soon after that. One of the last things she said to me before she stopped talking was—" And then he stopped. He said nothing for a long time. Then he said, "She said, 'I'll miss you.'"

This is the kind of thing that happens at meeting sometimes. In the silence that followed I thought of the man's wife dying in his arms, and suddenly the long, complicated poem I've been struggling with, about how in 1951 Senator Henry Cabot Lodge, who was a great Francophile, and his friend General de Lattre of France persuaded the American legislature to supply napalm and other arms to the French forces in Vietnam, seemed not worth doing. I don't want to know about evil via poetry. I don't want to spread the knowledge of evil. I just want to know about love. At the end of meeting, the clerk, Donna, said, "Do we have any visitors?" Someone from North Carolina said he was visiting from North Carolina. And then Donna said, "Okay, are there any almost messages?"

This is often my favorite part of meeting. An almost message is something somebody was on the verge of saying during silent meeting but for one reason or another didn't say, but the pressure to say it is still there.

This time a young woman in a brown short-sleeved dress said, "I sat down here an hour ago and there was nothing in my mind. I'd rushed to get here and there was just a jumble of stuff in my head that I'm supposed to be doing, a little to-do list for Sunday. And then in the silence a word came to me, and the word was 'unprepared.' I turned it over in my mind. I wasn't prepared for meeting. I had nothing to say. And then I thought, But isn't this the essence of Quakerism? We're not supposed be prepared. We're supposed to sit here and wait for what's true to come."

She said some more things I don't remember, and then she sat down, and I thought, She's right, the key sometimes is not to be prepared. Wait and see. Don't prepare for wars by having huge military bases all over the world, four hundred bases. Don't prepare for terrorists by creating a homeland bureaucracy. Don't expect people to hate one another. Wait and see what happens.

Then there were announcements. A film about sustainable agriculture was scheduled for Wednesday, and the knitting committee was going to be knitting blankets for sale, the proceeds to go for the furnace fund. They're thinking ahead to winter. Then everyone went into the other room to eat and have coffee.

Afterward I drove to Planet Fitness listening to the song about Darfur, by Mattafix. It's sung by a British man, Marlon Roudette, who has an extraordinary maple-sugar voice. At first I thought he was a woman. "Where others turn and sigh, you shall rise," he says.

Chevron discovered oil in the Darfur region of Sudan in 1978. In 1979, the CIA installed a friendly governor in Darfur, and the Carter administration began sending weapons and money to Jaafar Nimeiry, Sudan's president, who allowed the United States to build military bases in the country. Reagan sent more weapons and proclaimed that President Nimeiry, a murderous dictator, was a great friend to America—the CIA loved him because he was anti-Qaddafi. The result of our years of military assistance and meddling was a brutal civil war and a catastrophe of refugees and starvation. If you corrupt a government with money, weapons, and covert advisors, people are going to die. That's why the CIA has to be abolished immediately. It takes no great insight to see this. "You don't have to be extraordinary, just forgiving," sings Marlon Roudette.

YOU CAN'T INCLUDE IT ALL. You might think, I'll write a poem and it will have every good thing in it, and every bad thing, and every middling thing—it'll have Henry

Cabot Lodge and clouds and eggplant and Chuck Berry and the new flavor of Tom's of Maine toothpaste and bantam roosters and gas stations and seafoam-green Vespa scooters and the oversalting of rural roads—but it doesn't work. I've tried. As soon as the poem becomes longer than two pages, it stops being a poem and becomes something else. The longest poem I ever wrote came out in 1980 in a journal, now forgotten, not well known even then, called *Bird Effort*, which is the name of a Jackson Pollock painting. In the same issue was a poem by John Hall Wheelock, who had recently died—a friend and confidant of Sara Teasdale's who produced a glorious posthumous oral autobiography. Really, if you want to know about kindness and poetry in the twentieth century you should immediately read John Hall Wheelock's memoir. It was published a while ago by the University of South Carolina Press.

My long poem was called "Clouding Up" and it went on for two and a half pages. It was mostly about clouds. There was something in it about the Cloudboys and the Nimbians, I wince to remember. It was a poem I'd written in college. My creative writing teacher, a taciturn but fair-minded man, wrote, "I'm a bit baffled by this. To be frank, it's boring."

Well, yes, it was boring. But I was undeterred, and I sent it to fifteen places, and *Bird Effort* published it, and after that I wrote much shorter poems.

I've written three more poems about clouds since then. I can't get enough of them. I am drawn to describe them even though I know it's futile. They're different every day.

Debussy liked clouds. The first movement of his *Nocturnes* is called "Nuages." He also liked sunken cathedrals. He died when he was fifty-five.

I'M PARKED by the salt pile now. It sits here all summer, waiting for winter, when it will be dribbled out onto the roads and sometimes poison the roots of the trees.

All systems go. Boink. I'm ready. Thanks. Good.

Greetings, this is Chowder's Poetry Slurp, and I'm here to welcome you to another show in which we talk about the world of freelance hydroponics. I'm Paul Chowder, your harbormaster, confidant, and co-conspirator. And I hope that you will sit back and close your eyes and just let the poetry wash over you. Just let it pass over you in a lethal tide of poetical merriment. You are the sunken cathedral, my friend. This is PRI, Public Radio International.

"The Sunken Cathedral" is the name of a piece for solo piano by Claude Debussy. The experts say that it is based on a Breton folktale about the lost cathedral city of Ys—rhymes with "cease"—which allegedly sank beneath the waves one day when a woman stole the key to the seawall and the floodgates opened. But the experts don't know what they're talking about in this case. They're making it up. I've found this to be true over and over—the experts often don't know anything useful, really. First all women should have breast X-rays once a year and then, no, that's bad. First women should take hormone pills after menopause, then no.

First we should eat eggs. Then, no, eggs are bad because they have cholesterol. Then, no, eggs are good because they give you good cholesterol. And the advice is offered with such arrogant assurance. Roz's radio show is undermining some of that arrogance, and that's a good thing.

I talked to Gene, my editor, today, and when he asked I told him that I was making steady progress on my book of prosaic plums and that I now had a title for it: *Misery Hat*. I've sat on that poem all these years. It hurt that Peter Davison rejected it, and I turned against it and forgot about it. But I read it recently and thought it had some reasonably good turns, S-turns. Dryden has a nice passage about the French way of praising the turns in Virgil and Ovid: "*Delicat et bien tourné* are the highest commendation which they bestow on somewhat which they think a masterpiece."

Forget it, never mind, it doesn't matter.

"*Misery Hat*," said my editor. "Interesting title." I knew he didn't like it. I could hear that slight catch in his voice. But he's happy with me right now because *Only Rhyme* is still selling.

YOU THINK this is all a game, don't you? Well, it isn't. It's serious. I helped my dog Smacko into the car—he resists getting in the back seat and he's a little stiff these days—and I drove to Fort McClary with my music on shuffle. The Gap Band came on, singing "Early in the Morning." I hadn't really listened to the words before. For years, bizarrely, I paid almost no attention to the words in pop songs, even in Beatles songs. I heard them, and I could sometimes recite them, but I didn't care what they were about—they were just semi-random vocalizations over a chordal groove that I could move my head to like a wobble-headed figure on a cabbie's dashboard. Now I pay attention to the words. "Got to get up early in the morning, to find me another lover."

Then Fountains of Wayne came on, playing "All Kinds of Time." Holy shit, is that a good song. What a great undulating guitar thing in the middle. Shit! Apparently Collingwood, one of the songwriting pair of fountains, has or had a drinking problem—well, who wouldn't after singing a song as good as this one? He managed to catch the moment nobody has ever caught, the suspended hopeful moment as the quarterback is looking for a receiver, the most poignant and killing moment in football. There are some great chords, and Collingwood is able to control his falsetto notes, and the whole thing is just total genius. The quarterback knows that no one can touch him now. He's strangely at ease. The play is going to end in a sack—we realize it, gathered around the wide-screen TV—and then this slow wavy-gravy warble of a guitar solo comes on that is like the look of a football in flight—the football that he hasn't yet thrown—and it's totally mystical and soul-shaking. Power pop is the name given to Fountains of Wayne's style of music, it seems—but whatever it's called, they are great songwriters and they deserve thanks.

Roz's old blue Corolla was in the parking lot when I got to Fort McClary. She was sitting inside reading a new

New Yorker. All those years of *New Yorker*s that came when we were living together. She would read the articles. I flipped through, checking out the poems and laughing at the cartoons—some of the cartoons. And meanwhile the magazine got thinner. There was that terrible period a few years ago, after the crash, when there were almost no ads. Monsanto was on the back cover for a while—Monsanto, for goodness' sake, who wanted to inject cows with growth hormones so that their bony overtaxed bodies would rev up and create ungodly udderfuls of milk until they mooed to the skies for relief and their hooves rotted in the muck of their tight stalls. Monsanto actually had the gall to sue a dairy up in Portland, Maine—Oakhurst Dairy—to stop them from saying on the label that Oakhurst milk had no artificial bovine growth hormones, even though it was just a fact. Monsanto is evil, truly evil.

Roz hugged me and hugged our dog—it was our dog for a while, now it's my dog again—and she said happy birthday. She was wearing a light cotton sweatery thing I hadn't seen before, and a soft scarf that I knew from way back. I asked her how she was doing. "Okay, how about you?"

"Doing fine," I said. "The washing machine finally died, but I've kind of gotten into using the laundromat. Shall we clamber over the rocks? You know, the way we used to?" I gave it a Mick Jagger inflection and she smiled.

We led Smacko down to the shore and smelled the seaweed and looked out at the boats for a while. There were some drops of rain. We were a bit awkward with each other, I have to say, or maybe it was that the stones were unusually slippery—we'd lost some of our wonted familiarity. She told me she was working on a show about synthetic thyroid pills. Then we went back and I invited her out of the rain into my superclean car. She got the sandwiches and I opened the picnic basket. She'd brought a demi bottle of champagne to celebrate, which was awfully nice of her. The cork blew out the open window and we took bites of her egg salad. It was the best egg salad sandwich ever, and I said so. She'd also made a lemony beets-and-greens creation. I offered her some carrots and she crunched one, making an enormous sound.

"So what are you up to?" she asked.

I told her I'd bought a guitar and was learning some chords. "I think I'm done with poems for the moment. I'm writing songs now."

"Can I hear one?"

"Not yet. But I vacuumed the car in your honor."

She looked around. "Very nice. I have to say—" She hesitated. "It smells a tiny bit like smoke. Are you smoking cigarettes?"

"No no no. Cigars."

"Oh, baby. Why?"

"I tried a corncob pipe and it was no good for me. Before that, I tried a can of Skoal, and it made me ill. I've stopped drinking. No beer, no Yukon Jack, no Tyrconnell. I need some new tongue-loosening addiction."

"I can't imagine you as a cigar smoker—I don't want to imagine you as a cigar smoker."

"It's just a phase. It's my brown period." I stuffed the plastic bag that my sandwich came in into the picnic basket. "Are you still on friendly terms with that doctor dude?"

"Harris." She nodded.

"Isn't 'Harris' kind of a needless encumbrance? Does he really know you and understand you?"

Roz gave me a look. "Progress is being made," she said. "There are complications."

"Because I know you and I love you," I said. "It's my birthday and I can say that."

"Then what about that woman in Pennsylvania?"

"You'd moved out, you were gone!" I said. "It was brief and fleeting and completely wrong in every way." Several years ago I had an untidy interlude with a poet from Lehigh University, and I'd made the mistake of telling Roz, hoping it might make her jealous and bring her back.

"I moved out because you were being impossible," Roz said. "We had no money and you were singing in the barn all day long."

"I know. I'm sorry."

She looked at her hands. I made a big sigh. Smack whimpered from the back and Roz gave him some of her sandwich.

"Cigars," she said. "Not good."

"I'll stop smoking them if you move back in with me."

"Please, I'm serious. The show is so much work, and— I wasn't going to tell you this—but I'm anemic. I'm very anemic. I have pica."

"Oh baby, how absolutely awful." I moved the picnic basket clumsily so I could hold her hand. "What's pica?"

"Do you remember how I used to have those terrible periods that just went on and on?"

I said I certainly did.

"Well, they're worse now," Roz said. "They last more than a week and I go through boxes of ultra tampons. It's a festival of gore every month. I haven't been sleeping, because when you're anemic you don't sleep. You just sit up eating poppy seeds and anything crunchy. Sesame seeds—I eat tubs of sesame seeds. And dry oatmeal. Sometimes I want to eat the whole sidewalk. That's what pica is. For instance." She pointed. "See that big rock? To me it looks chewable. I want to eat that rock. That's how messed up I am."

"Oh my goodness," I said. "Are you taking iron pills?"

"Yes, yes, but they don't agree with me. I've been eating masses of collard greens, though."

"What does the gynecologist say?"

"She says—" Roz started to cry.

"Sweetie!" I said.

"Don't worry, it's not cancer. But it sure is a pain." She wiped her eyes with her napkin and took a breath. "I'll be fine. I have to go now. I have to read a stack of research papers. We have a show coming up on colonoscopies. Harris thinks they're a false religion, that most of them are unnecessary, and he's pretty convincing."

"Good, because nobody's going to be poking around in

my bottom. A doctor snuck a thermometer in there when I was five years old and it was horrible. Humiliating."

Roz smiled. "I'm sorry to hear that," she said.

"Ah, don't be, water under the bridge."

"Well, happy birthday, honey." She kissed me on the cheek and drove off in her sporty battered car.

Nine

ROZ LOOKED PALE, now that I think of it. She's working too hard. I sent her an email thanking her for the egg salad sandwich. "I'm worried about you," I said. "Call me if I can do anything. Thank you for the picnic. Love -P. PS Forgot to say—great show on spinal fusion surgery! PPS I'm having problems writing lyrics. Only if you have time—can you think of some random three-word phrases, each using only one-syllable words?"

When Roz first moved in with me, I dusted off the traveling sprinkler and showed her what it looked like. I showed her how it worked, how you hooked up the hose to its fundament and the water surged in and up through its bowels and out the two twirly wands and how you could adjust the angle of the spray that came from the rusted ends of the wands. She lifted it and remarked at how heavy it was. She was delighted by it in her good-natured way. "It's so simple," she said.

I don't want to say that a traveling sprinkler is the best way to water a lawn, because it isn't. The best way to water a lawn is to live in a place where there's enough rain, and when there are hot, dry months the lawn just stops growing and gets dusty. That's how you should water a lawn. But if you want to have a big garden party and you want really green grass for it—say you want to have a wedding or a game of badminton and you want the grass to be very healthy and strong to hold up under all those happy, playful feet—then you lay out the hose course. You make the track. It's better than the Disney Monorail. It's better than the water slide made of plastic.

You lay that hose out like you're squirting icing on a coffee cake, in a big set of repeating S's. You can't make the turns too sharp—nothing can be abrupt or "discontinuous," as they say in Algebra II. The brilliance of the whole thing comes in its ability to ride its source of power. It's a serious cast-iron machine.

When we first got together, Roz had wanted to have a baby, and like the selfish dumbass I was I'd said, "Not now"—which meant not ever.

I'M LISTENING to a song called "Jacuzzi Games," by Loco Dice. There are no words. A woman makes soft but unfeigned-sounding murmurs and purrs of sexual pleasure over a good beat, with some added echo. The bassline doesn't change. I've been working on my traveling sprinkler poem. When I'm fiddling with a poem it's better not to have any words coming in the headphones. But then I sometimes reach a point when I'm totally absorbed. Then I can play any song at all, words or not. I don't hear the words as words. Those are the best times. I can be listening to Springsteen singing "Pink Cadillac" in a shady spot on Inigo Road and be writing about sitting in a treehouse reading William Cullen Bryant's poem "A Hymn of the Sea" while smoking a huge, nasty cigar from Federal Cigar, as I did yesterday. "A Hymn of the Sea" is in an ornate edition with a hundred engravings and my grandfather's name written in pencil in the front. He wanted to be a poet and didn't quite make it. My great-grandfather wrote light verse. I come from a long line of extremely minor poets.

My grandfather smoked pipes. Stéphane Mallarmé smoked cigars. Both of them died of throat cancer. Yesterday I went into Federal Cigar and I said to the man at the register that I needed a really good powerful cigar—a cigar that would help me finish a book of poems. "You want something full-bodied," he said. He led me into the silent humidor room with its wall of dense brown cigars in boxes looking like old leather-bound books of unread sermons in a historic house in the Yorkshire moors, and he said, "Do you want strong but smooth, or do you want something that will really—" He trailed off.

"I want something that blows my head off," I said. "Something that really mops the floor with me."

He nodded and handed me a Fausto Esteli. "This'll do it," he said.

I bought two Faustos, a Viaje Summerfest, a Fuente Opus X, and a sampler pack of five miscellaneous cigars in a plastic bag.

BEFORE I BEGAN driving around in my car last year, I stopped writing poems altogether for a little while. I think I know the reason why. It's not because I'm "blocked." What a misleading term, "writer's block," based as it is on a false physical analogy. No, it's because my anthology, *Only Rhyme*, was actually selling. Not selling hugely well, but selling fairly well in a steady sort of way. It's used as a textbook in some big southwestern universities, who—I'm just guessing—employ it for their own reactionary purposes. And that is a very good thing for me, because life is expensive. The IRS isn't happy with me. I took the first royalty check and spent it right away and made no estimated payments. I gave a hundred dollars to the War Resisters League and fifty dollars to Common Dreams.

But the minor success of *Only Rhyme* meant that whenever I thought about a poem I was working on, part of me looked at it with a jaundiced eye, the way a professional anthologist would. I asked myself, Is what I have made today good enough to anthologize somewhere? And no, of course it wasn't. Most poems aren't anthologizable. Most poems are just poems.

So I had to learn to forget. I eventually did, more or less. I'm not an anthologist, I am a free man!

SECOND THOUGHTS about the title. I called my editor back. "Sorry to bother you, Gene," I said. "It's just that I sensed you weren't crazy about *Misery Hat*. Am I right?"

Gene said, "To be perfectly honest, the word 'misery' stops me. It isn't exactly the sellingest word to put on the cover of a book. Stephen King did it, but I'm not sure it's the right move for you."

I told him that I'd been writing a lot in my car. Maybe the book could be called *Car Poems*?

He said, "Hmm, maybe, maybe." I could tell he didn't like *Car Poems* much, either.

"How about *Listen to the Warm*? I'm joking, that's a book by Rod McKuen."

"Don't fret yourself over the title," Gene said. "We can get to that later. Just write the poems."

I moaned and said, "Honestly, and I shouldn't tell you this, but I'm not much of a poet these days. I was sitting in Quaker meeting the other day and I realized I didn't want to write sad complicated poems, I wanted to write sad simple songs. In other words, I want to write sad poems that are made happier by being singable."

"Well then, write them, sing them," Gene said. "Sad simple poems are perfectly acceptable. Come on, now."

"You're right. Thanks, Gene."

"And don't be afraid of putting a little sex in them, the way you used to. That always spices things up. Chastity is for whores."

PEOPLE OFTEN CONFUSE the words "bassoon" and "oboe," as Tim did. I think it's because the word "oboe" sounds sort of like a sound emanating from a bassoon: *oboe*. But the two instruments look very different. The oboe is small and black and your eyes pop out staringly when you play it, and it's used all the time in movie soundtracks during plaintive moments, whereas the bassoon is a brown snorkel that pokes up at an angle above the orchestra. You almost feel you could play it underwater while the violists and oboists gasp and splutter.

I used to really want to be a snorkler. I had black swim fins, and my grandparents took us on a cruise of some Greek islands—oh, forget it. Not now.

I'm down to the nub end of this Fausto cigar. I actually singed an eyebrow hair relighting it, if that's possible. Sometimes a cigar is just a bassoon.

When you played a long tone on the bassoon, the veins would come out in your neck and in your forehead, and your hands would feel thick with an oversupply of blood, but still you would keep playing the note, pumping it fuller and fuller, because the note was everything—this hump-shaped swell of non-music was all that you were aiming to achieve. It was premusical music. It taught control. Control was everything.

I was determined to become the greatest bassoonist that the state of New Hampshire, that the world, had ever known. I was very ambitious back then.

Billy Brown always knew the weeks when I had concentrated on long tones, because those were the weeks in which I sounded especially bad. The practicing broke me and exhausted me and hurt my jaw. I was completely devoted to this expensive folded cylinder of maplewood with the metal U-turn at the bottom. The spit gathered there like a noxious underground lake where a spit Kraken lived. It was a postwar Heckel, made in Wiesbaden, Germany. It came in a wooden crate, like a plain coffin, with the word FRAGILE stenciled on it.

Ten

R OZ WROTE that she's feeling better. She sent me a whole list of three-word lines, including "crack the nut," "drop the pants," "shake the stick," and "learn to dance."

What do I know about sex? People taking their clothes off and fucking their way around the house? Fifty Shades of Marvin Fucking Gaye?

Roz was—no doubt is—a wonderful sexpot. We used to pour each other tiny glasses of Tyrconnell and put them on our bedside tables. Tyrconnell was our sex drink. Let me tell you, the Irish did a lot more than save civilization. The first time she sipped it, Roz described how it tasted. Her first sip, she said, tasted of primeval forest. Then the second sip: slate patio. Third sip: patio furniture with slippery steps down to the garden. Fourth sip: meat, meat with heavy, dark green vegetable matter on an earthenware platter. Fifth sip:

swallowing the platter. Sixth sip: recovery, bisque-colored envelopes.

Sometimes along with the Tyrconnell we used to read each other Victorian pornography, skipping the incestuous parts, which isn't easy, because there is an astonishing amount of incest in Victorian pornography. Why is there so much incest? Aunts, uncles, mothers, fathers, sisters, brothers— was sex with near relations really the be-all and end-all of the era of Palmerston and Disraeli? When it isn't incest, it's birchings and floggings and nuns and priests. Nunnery stories can be good, though. Dirty doings in the confessional can be good. And harem stories can be good.

I FEEL LIKE a traveling sprinkler that's gotten off the hose. I don't know where I'm going. I'm unprepared. Good for me. I could make some extra money this summer shrink-wrapping boats. I should do that.

I want it all to seem easier for me than it is. I want people to think that I'm a fountain of verbal energy. I've never really been a fountain.

There's an excellent children's poem about a drinking fountain. The poet's name is Marchette Chute. I was fascinated by the drinking fountains in high school, with the warm, suspect water that came up past the steam pipes. There was usually some flesh-colored gum lying like a tiny naked baby Jesus in the drain. I was thirsty, and yet the water burbled up and just barely crested past the germ-laden part.

At a mattress store where I worked briefly, there was a drinking fountain that offered very cold refrigerated water. I used to stay up all night writing poems and then go to work hauling mattresses around, and to stay alert I would put a Reese's peanut butter cup in my mouth and start chewing it and then take a sip of water and the cold water would mix with the chocolate and the sweet peanut butter and the two would help each other. Cold fountain water through a Reese's cup, nothing better.

I used to want to start a museum of the water fountain. I saw an old water fountain from Paris in an antique store. I wanted to amass a collection and open a museum that would be listed in one of those books of eccentric museums. You've seen that book, *Little Museums*? Because when you consider it, a drinking fountain is probably the most important single piece of plumbing that you drink from without a glass or a cup. Can you think of any other piece of plumbing that allows you to drink from an arch of cold water, when it's functioning correctly at least? I think you'd be hard pressed. "I turn it up," writes Marchette Chute. "The water goes / And hits me right / Upon the nose. / I turn it down / To make it small / And don't get any / Drink at all." A classic poem.

After I first met Roz, I called her up at work and said, "Roz, I have the most terrible hangover, do you have any recommendations?" She said, "Yes. Go to the drinking fountain and bend down and go into one of those altered states of hypnotic drinking, where your throat just goes *ng, ng, ng, ng* and you think you'll never breathe again but will simply drink at this fountain for your whole life." I said, "Okay, I'll try it." I called her back and said it had helped. That's how we got together.

WHAT IT COMES down to, for the working poet, is this. Either you can go have the eggs Benedict at the place with the copper tables, and it'll cost you nine dollars, plus a big tip— sometimes as much as five dollars in tip if you occupy a whole booth for a long time, wearing a big pair of headphones when it's crowded—or you can make a sandwich for yourself, and wash an apple, and cut some carrots, and eat it in the car, and it'll cost maybe two dollars. You can eat five times as many meals if you don't go to the place with the copper tables.

On the other hand, it's helpful to be around people. You can listen to the jokey fat men flirt with the older waitress.

"More coffee, my good sir?"

"Yes, please, precious, and on second thought I'll have another side of home fries."

"Aren't you a big spender today."

"I don't pay alimony and I don't pay child support. I've got all the money in the world."

"How nice for you."

I think my brakes are really going. They're soft and they make a scraping sound. My penis is soft and it doesn't make a scraping sound.

What I miss about Roz is of course her lady parts and her pleasure frown and her funny talk. She has a kind of genius for coming up with odd but friendly words for things. She's a namer of unnameables. But the main thing I miss is how nice she is to people. When her friend Lucy's father died she made a card and baked her a loaf of cranberry bread. She's full of ideas about what other people would want. She's the opposite of selfish. Her unselfishness was a revelation to me. She was, and is, full of this quality that I've come to take seriously, which is lovingkindness. Lovingkindness, all one word.

I tried for a while to get her to come to Quaker meeting with me, because in many ways she's an extremely Quakerly person, but she didn't want to. Her mother is Irish Catholic and her father is Russian Jewish, and in her case that mixture resulted in an incredibly nice human being who has no interest even in a religion as disorganized and uncodified as Quakerism.

I feel sad that we've become so formal with each other now. But that's what happens. We're more relaxed with each other via email, which is a bad sign.

HELLO MY TINY MUMBLES, welcome to the Chowder Hour of Razorwire and Shiny Festal Splendor. Glad you could join me. I've found a new chord on the guitar and with it I've written part of a song called "Love Is an Amazing Magnet." I've also embarked on a song about doctors, inspired by Roz's radio show. I stayed up late rhyming "Nexium" and "thyroxin," and I wrote way too many verses, some of which are:

The doctor's in
The nurse is hot
Swab some cotton
Cause you're getting a shot

Tell me a symptom
I'll tap your vein
I'll pap your smear
And scan your brain

Crap in a baggie
Piss in a cup
Another appointment
For a follow-up

Tubes in your pipes
Wires in your head
Keep you alive
Till you're practically dead

The chorus is "Oh babe, I can't wait, for you all day." I'm going to play Roz some of my songs, and then she's going to say good-bye to Harris the doctor and get back together with me. Because I know her. It's time. But what if I try and it doesn't happen? Then I'll be sad—much sadder than if I hadn't tried, because it really will be the end.

Eleven

THE GUITAR LESSON did not go well. My fingers didn't want to cooperate and I had some trouble with tuning. I tightened the E string too hard and snapped it—classic stupidity—and the teacher, who was a pleasant aging hipster sort of gentleman, showed me how to replace it. That was helpful. He also showed me "Blowin' in the Wind," the proper way to strum it. That was a good song to start with, because Dylan's singing is sometimes a little shaky—not as shaky as mine, but he's no Harry Nilsson. I asked the teacher who his favorite singer was. "That's an impossible question," he said. But he said he liked people like Steve Winwood.

Quaker meeting is in eight minutes. I'm parked in a space across the street. I don't want to go in, because I stink of cigar. But I am going to go in anyway, because I like the goodness in these people and I always feel better after I've gone.

———

AND NOW MEETING is over and I'm back in the car. One of the elders, Chase—the man who sang "How Can I Keep from Singing?"—was shaking hands at the door when I went in. Meeting was crowded and there were a number of young children. I sat down in an empty stretch of pew far enough away from the next person, a filmmaker I knew slightly, so that I thought he wouldn't smell me. I put my finger through my key ring and closed my fist around my car key. People were smiling and looking around, as they do while latecomers arrange themselves. The last to arrive were a mother and her three children, followed by an older man in a white shirt who sat next to me. He was a bit out of breath from hurrying, and I heard his breathing gradually slow down. I listened to the clock for a while and thought about how many people were wearing plaid. One woman had gotten her hair cut short in a way that looked very good. I closed my eyes and felt that time was moving faster, maybe a little too fast. The windows were open, and the door was open, and the sound of a passing car traveled slowly through the room. After that there was stillness. A little boy held his mother's gold watch, turning it in his hands and smiling a secret smile. Then the silence changed and deepened, and for several seconds it was perfect and I felt a sort of ecstasy. Then someone shifted and adjusted a pillow for her back, and I could feel my pew bend when the man next to me crossed his legs. Again a car sound poured softly in through the windows and out the open door. We were permeable. We were a meeting permeated with openness.

After fifteen minutes Donna the clerk said, "We want to thank the children for worshipping with us. Can they shake hands around the room?" The children pushed themselves off their pews with serious faces and shook hands with the people who sat in the first rows of pews that faced the center of the room. There was a shockingly beautiful girl of about six with a barrette that was not doing a good job of holding her hair. She nodded politely as she shook the knobby hand of the oldest of the elders, a thin, tenderly smiling woman who wore hearing-aid headphones. Then the children left and I listened to them thumping down the stairs to the basement. Muffledly I heard the teacher call, "Don't touch the stuff on the table yet!"

Then again the clock and the silence. I looked down for a long time and bent over, leaning my elbows on my knees, still holding my car key, and then I remembered the helpful tip about posture and I imagined the hooks in my rib cage and sat up. I opened my eyes and I saw that nobody was smiling now and many people had their eyes closed. Time seemed to be going even faster, as if it were a train picking up speed. Many minutes went by. I wondered who would speak. Nobody did. I looked at the clock. It said ten after eleven. I wanted someone to speak. Surely someone would offer testimony about something. But I noticed that the woman who sometimes talked about her birdbath wasn't there. She was often the first to speak, and once she spoke others did.

Silence was all very well, but in order to feel the silence you need a few words.

I didn't think that I should say anything, because I'd said something about chickens the last time I went. On the other hand, someone should speak. I checked the clock. There were only ten minutes of meeting left. A woman got up and I thought she was going to say something, but she just left to arrange the after-meeting food in the other room. Please someone say something!

I WANTED TO TELL the Quakers about Debussy's sunken cathedral. I kept formulating an opening in my head. "A little more than a hundred years ago, a composer named Claude Debussy wrote a piece for piano called 'The Sunken Cathedral.' He was a man with a big forehead who loved the sea. His most famous piece of music is called *La Mer*, the sea. And in one of his early songs he set to music a poem by Verlaine with the words 'The sea is more beautiful than cathedrals.' But when he wrote his tenth piano prelude, 'The Sunken Cathedral,' 'La Cathédrale Engloutie,' he was no longer young and he was harassed by money worries and he had symptoms of the cancer that would kill him and he was thinking that life hadn't turned out quite the way he had expected." I wanted to tell them all this, but I couldn't because it was late, and it was really too much to say in meeting. I always felt a little like a godless impostor among these genuinely worshipful folk.

There were only four minutes of meeting left. I hoped that the woman with the big white hair would say something— she often spoke at the very end of meeting. She was sitting with a slight almost smile and her eyes were closed. Everyone seemed content with the silence. I've been reading a biography of Gerard Manley Hopkins, and I thought maybe I should say something about Hopkins's articles on sunsets for *Nature* magazine. After the Krakatoa explosion, Hopkins wrote three articles for *Nature* describing the unusual colors of the sunset that he'd meticulously recorded in his notebooks. But there was no time to say that, and it was too raw, really, to be a message anyway. Then again, at 11:29 a.m., I thought I absolutely must stand and tell them about the sunken cathedral. I wanted to say that Debussy played enormous still chords and out of them you can see the smoky blue water and the decayed pillars of the ruined church and the long blue fishes steering themselves down the nave and poking their snouts at the lettucey seaweeds. I wanted to say that in 1910 Debussy felt a great disappointment. That he wrote a friend that sometimes he wished he was a sponge at the bottom of the sea—*éponge*, a usefully squeezable word in French. But then he came up with this piece of music, the tenth prelude, and in it he created a great shadowy still place underwater, this place of peacefulness where when you listen to the music you can go and watch the medieval fishes swim. I wanted to say that he'd always wanted to *noyer le ton*, to drown the tonality, and he did it by closing the lid of the piano and holding down the sustain pedal and letting the elements of the chords pile up. I wanted to say, "He was sick, he couldn't play the piano as virtuosically then as he had in music school, when he could noodle for hours and amaze his fellow students with harmonies they'd never heard before, but out of his sense of disappointment and out of his money worries and out of his new sense of his own mortality he built an ancient crumbling lost ruin that nobody had known about, and we can hear it and see it hanging there or standing there on the seafloor in the silence." I didn't say it.

Then it was one minute after eleven-thirty and Donna turned to shake hands with the man next to her, and she smiled, and everyone smiled and shook hands with the people around them. Donna thanked us for choosing to worship there and a visitor introduced herself. She was from Eliot, Maine. A woman announced that the soup kitchen needed volunteers. Another woman reminded us that a man was giving a talk on solar power on Wednesday evening. Then two members grasped the handles on the large wooden panel that closed off meeting from the room where the potluck food was, and pulled it up, not without effort because it was more than two hundred years old and stuck in its frame, and when they'd pushed it up above six feet, another person propped it into place with a long pole. I nodded hello to the old man and to several others and walked out into the marvelous morning sunlight. The woman from Eliot was behind me. "You're a visitor," I said.

"Yes."

I shook her hand. Something made me say, "Most of the

time there are messages. Usually people say a few things during meeting. It's not always totally silent."

"Oh," she said. "Do people generally park on the street?"

I said that generally they did, yes.

"Because I didn't know and I parked up there." She pointed to her car in one of the spaces in the small lot behind the meetinghouse. "After I did I wasn't sure if that was all right."

"Oh, it's perfectly fine," I said. I waved my keys at her. "Have a nice Sunday."

"You, too." She waved her keys at me.

I walked to my car and lit up the stub of my Opus X cigar and smoked it until the label began to burn. It's made in the Dominican Republic and wrapped with leaves grown from Cuban seeds.

Twelve

THIS IS PAUL CHOWDER, sitting in a plastic chair. I want—I want—I want to tell you something new. I feel that I have a new thing.

What is it when you have an urge to produce something, to make something, and it almost doesn't matter whether it's good or not? When I was a little kid, in first grade, there was a project that we had to do in class. We were supposed to make a holiday wreath. It was to be made from a bent coat hanger, tied with the plastic wrap that came from the shrouds that went over your clothes when you picked them up from the dry cleaners.

The strange thing was that the dry cleaners that my father went to used blue-tinted plastic. On the appointed day I brought the blue plastic sheet to school. But I noticed that everybody else's dry cleaner plastic was clean and clear. Mine was blue, and theirs was clear. I was horrified by the idea that

I'd brought in the wrong raw material. The teacher gave me some extra clear plastic, but there wasn't enough for a whole wreath. "You can take pieces of clear plastic and do part of the wreath," she said gently, "and then alternate with the blue plastic." I shook my head. Everybody else's wreath was knotted with thick luscious densely packed bow-ties of clear plastic. I didn't want to finish the blue-striped wreath, but I did. It was a shaming disappointment. My mother wanted to hang it on the door but I said no. And yet why was I raising a fuss? It doesn't make any sense. What were we doing making plastic Christmas wreaths, anyway?

This morning I woke up at four a.m. and read the beginning of Medea Benjamin's book on drone warfare. Benjamin talks about meeting a thirteen-year-old girl who was begging on the road near the border between Afghanistan and Pakistan. In 2002, a missile hit her house while she was outside carrying a bucket of water; it killed her mother and her two brothers. Her name was Roya. Her father, a vendor of sweets, had survived, but he did not speak. I got up and watched a video of Medea Benjamin telling the story to an audience at a library. She said that Roya's father had carefully gathered pieces of his wife and his sons from the tree near their house and buried them. Oh, Jesus. Roya. That poor girl. Her poor father. Their lives completely demolished. I was traumatized and angry—angry at General Atomics, the company that makes drones, angry at George W. Bush, angry at Barack Obama for increasing the drone attacks fivefold after he was elected. I paced the kitchen for a while feeling powerless and ineffectual. At least Tim is writing his book.

I WENT TO PLANET FITNESS and had a long session on the elliptical trainer. By the time I was done, the parking lot was crowded with cars and I couldn't remember where I'd parked. I walked up and down and then I started singing, "I lost my car in the parking lot, I lost my car in the parking lot." Was it a song? Yes, in a way it was.

Once I found my car, which was parked way over to the right, I started home. I saw a street sweeper—a big yellow street sweeper with an invisible pilot high up in the cab. It looked like it was driving itself. I love street sweepers, I always have, even more than garbage trucks. I love the way the big rear roller turns inward against the forward movement of the machine, flinging the mess that the front bristles have dug away from the curb up into some inner holding area. "Sweeper" was one of the first words I said, according to my mother's stories. "Sweeper" and "lung lord." "Lung lord" was how I said "lawnmower."

I lit a Ramones cigar, from Honduras—one of the shorter cigars in the grab bag—and I pressed the button on my recorder and sang, "Street sweeper baby, coming down the street. Spinning those bristles and keeping it neat." That's definitely a song. When I got home I grabbed my guitar and went up to the barn and clutched out a few chords and matched the chords to the melody, and I was in business, in a primitive sort of way. It was very windy and the barn creaked—I could hear the joists moving and twisting—but I ignored the wind's white eyeballs. I spent the morning recording snippets of songs, and then I took Smack for a walk in the park near Strawbery Banke, where all the historic houses are. Strawbery Banke, is there a song in Strawbery Banke? No. I looked across the water at the submarine base. What about a song about a burning submarine? "The submarine was burning, going up in smoke." No. "The sea warriors watched while their submarine burned." No, definitely not, because Chuck worked on submarines and it would make Nan unhappy if I wrote a song about Chuck's precious submarine.

Oh, but the guitar sounded good. I couldn't get over how good a D minor chord sounded on the guitar. Little old D minor. I once played a Mahler symphony with a D minor bassoon solo, big deal—Mahler's interminable Sixth Symphony. But this guitar D minor was different. By shifting two fingers you can go from a D minor to some other chord with a suspended something-or-other. D minor, then strange chord, then D minor again. So beautiful. "It's early morning and the rollers are rolling," I sang. "The rollers are rolling in the early morning."

Everything's different when you write a song. The rhymes sound different and they happen naturally, and the chords don't sound like the same chords played on a piano. Your fingers make choices for you. The guitar is your friend, helping you find chords you'd never have found on your own, and then those chords help you find tunes you'd never

have thought to sing. It's such a simple and glorious col-
laboration.

Is it possible to write a song about the beginnings of
the CIA? About the fetish of secrecy? I know a little secret
about the CIA. I bet you don't know this. I'm going to tell it
to you right now. The true founder of the CIA was a poet,
Archibald MacLeish. Well, that's not quite right. MacLeish
was one of the true founders, one of the early recruiters and
legitimizers.

When Franklin Roosevelt wanted to set up a bureau
of secret intelligence—this was in the summer of 1941—he
assigned the job of creating an intelligence agency to two
highly placed people. One was William Donovan, a
Republican lawyer who'd gone to Pearl Harbor to "inspect
the fleet" before it was attacked and gone to London to cook
up trouble and help set Europe ablaze. The other was FDR's
poet speechwriter, the man who'd won a Pulitzer Prize for
saying, with great self-importance, that a poem must not
mean but be: Archibald MacLeish. MacLeish had already
helped Wild Bill Donovan with some of his interventionist
speeches—they stayed up late in Donovan's place in New
York fashioning what Donovan would say on the radio about
how convoys of American destroyers should be protecting
British ships—and he was setting up a new propaganda
agency called the Office of Facts and Figures, and he was,
incidentally, Librarian of Congress. When Roosevelt wanted

an Office of Censorship to keep the lid on bad news, he put MacLeish on the board of directors. MacLeish wanted to be in control of all government information. He was fascinated by air power—the physical air power of bombing, and also the ideological air power of propagandistic radio. He wanted us in the war, but he wanted us to fight smart, at high altitude, with careful targeting and big new weapons made in democratic factories—to fight, above all, with the really big weapon, managed truth. Elizabeth Bishop wrote dismissively of MacLeish's "mellifluous and meaningless" speeches. The *Chicago Tribune* called him the Bald Bard of Balderdash.

In August 1941, Donovan and MacLeish met on a cool porch and sketched an organizational chart for a secret agency, and afterward MacLeish sent out telegrams to academicians of war planning, including William Langer at Harvard and James Phinney Baxter at Williams: "Colonel Donovan as coordinator of information is setting up a central intelligence service with which the Library of Congress is cooperating," MacLeish said in the telegrams. The war planners met, and one of MacLeish's librarians produced a long document titled "Proposal for a CENTRAL INTELLIGENCE SERVICE for the Federal Government Together with the Relationship of THE LIBRARY OF CONGRESS Thereto." It ended up being called the Office of Strategic Services, the OSS, and it did many counterproductive secret things during the war, some of which are still classified, and in 1945 Harry Truman formally abolished it and fired Donovan. But Archibald MacLeish carefully watched over the shreds of

OSS intelligence that were left, in his new job as assistant secretary of state, and then a few years later Truman realized he needed a spy service after all, in order to do battle with the evil Communist conspiracy as it was manifesting itself in Greece and Italy and Southeast Asia and everywhere else. Truman wanted to overthrow Communist leaders by spreading around bribe money and napalm and ammunition, so he reconstituted the OSS. But now it was called the Central Intelligence Agency, echoing MacLeish's original name. And some of MacLeish's young Yale protégés from Skull and Bones, including Cord Meyer and James Jesus Angleton, eventually became the CIA's senior paranoid poltergeists. So now you know. Archibald MacLeish was one of the original instigators and organizers of this bloated monstrosity of assassination and violent regime change and unaccountable underhanded ugliness and skullduggery. And drone warfare. Which is why Plato was right: poets should never get involved in politics.

Is there a song in that? Probably not. I don't want to know about evil, I just want to know about love. Stephen Fearing sang this song in 2007 in a hotel lobby in Paris. Listen to it on YouTube and you will be happy: www.youtube.com/watch?v=HiJjLdcFF6Y.

I so admire people who can sing. They tell their voice to go somewhere and it just goes there. Or they say, Don't go there, go almost there and swerve up into position at the last second. There's an unspeakable intelligence in what they're doing. No words can describe it.

I went out and spent twenty dollars on sushi at Fresh Market, and then I went to the chocolate factory on Hanover Street and bought dessert: some special pistachio bark sprinkled with chili powder and cayenne pepper and cinnamon. It has magical mood-altering properties, I think, and even if it doesn't it tastes good. On the ride home I got lucky when I was listening to my songs on shuffle: I came to something by Anna Nalick called "Breathe." I was sitting at a stoplight and suddenly there was an amazing woman singing in my ears about how life's like an hourglass glued to the table and what you have to do is breathe, just breathe. Something papery in me crumpled and I crunched my eyes closed and sang tunelessly along with Anna Nalick, and I listened to every word. The last time I'd thought about that song was back in 2009, when I was in a hotel room in Cincinnati after a reading.

It was so good that I tapped the genius icon, the little atom, to make a genius playlist from songs that iTunes in its wisdom thought were like "Breathe." The Weepies came on, another group I haven't thought about in a while, singing that the world spins madly on, and then came another good song that I'd forgotten, by Kate Earl, called "Melody." "Melody" is about how Kate Earl listens to songs all day long and she has nobody beside her to go ooh ooh ooh, but her skin is warm and her heart is full and the music is loud so her hips can swing. I bet they do—those woman's hips, those hourglass hips, they don't lie. I think "Melody" was a free single on iTunes one week, that's how I got it. And here Kate Earl was just singing it for me. I started to dance in the car, taking a right turn into my driveway. She says something very profound and simple: "Every missing piece of me, I can find in a melody."

This song is a wonder. There are sleighbells in the background for some reason, who can explain it?

Thirteen

NAN CAME SMILINGLY OVER with Raymond and I said, "Hi, folks," and sat them down at the kitchen table. I decanted the sushi onto plates and brought out the little soy sauce saucers so that we could each of us mix our own personal octane mix of wasabi. The best thing about sushi is the wasabi mustard—it clears your head like nothing else. We talked about the chickens for a while, and whether a fresh egg tastes different from an egg you get from the supermarket. Nan said that before she got the bantam rooster a hawk had killed two chickens, but the flyweight bantam is fierce and fearless and he protects them. Then I asked Raymond how his music was going. He said it was going okay. I asked him if he could show me how he made beats and he pulled his MPC beat-making machine from his backpack and we hooked it up to my computer speakers and he cycled through some of the presets and got a chesty kick drum going and made a quick eight-bar loop. It sounded excellent. Nan and I were rocking our heads, looking at each other with our eyebrows slightly raised while Raymond tapped on the rubber pads with his fingers and fiddled with dials.

"So Raymond," I said, after a while, "what would you suggest I get if I wanted to make music? Should I get one of these MPC things? I can't spend a huge amount of money."

"What kind of music do you see yourself making?" said Raymond, in a grown-up sort of way.

"Well, I bought a cheap guitar and I really like it"—I pointed at my Gibson Maestro, carelessly propped in a corner of the kitchen—"but really I'd kind of like to make a superfunky dance song that people would have to get up and dance to."

"There are basically two ways to go," said Raymond, "real analog hardware or software. I use both. Hardware's nice because you've got actual dials and faders and pads, but it's pricey. Do you have vocals?"

"Yes, I've got some vocals. Vocal fragments."

"Then you're going to need a good microphone and a USB audio interface. The Saffire 6 is good."

"His grandparents gave him some money for his education," Nan explained.

"Thank heaven for grandparents," I said. "My grandparents bought me a bassoon."

"A bassoon," said Raymond. "Do you still play?"

I said I'd sold it a long time ago. "And I have very limited means at the moment."

"Then you should just go with software. Get Logic. It'll cost you two hundred dollars and it's got tons of instruments."

"Okay." I began taking notes. "Logic."

"Yeah, you can pretty much do any bizarro thing you want with it. It's got a synth called Sculpture that makes glass and wood sounds, and sounds like bouncing marbles."

"Bouncing marbles," I said, longingly, writing it down.

Raymond pulled out his computer and showed me a song he'd been working on in Logic. The vocal tracks were blue and the other tracks were green. He touched the A key and showed me how he'd made a white-noise sweep. "There are vocals with these," he said, "but I've got them muted."

"Play some of the vocals," said Nan.

Raymond hesitated. "Mom, as you know, they're a tad explicit."

"Oh, go ahead," said Nan. "We don't mind being shocked, do we, Paul?"

"Let me quick listen first," said Raymond. I handed Nan the pistachio bark while Ray put on his huge studio headphones—they had a spiral cord—and he listened to his lyrics, moving his head to the side with the beat. He hit the space bar to stop the playback and grimaced. "I'm not sure. I'll play you a little bit of the chorus."

He played the chorus. It was something like "Baby I got

some beans in these jeans, I got some beans in these jeans!"
There was something else about "crucial fluids."

I laughed, slightly embarrassed for Nan. "That's good,"
I said. "Very catchy. Nice hook. Let's hear more."

"I've got another song that's less inappropriate." He
hunted in a folder for the file.

"This is wild and spicy," said Nan, meaning the chocolate.

Ray played us some of the other song. Something about
"My shoes don't want to fit and I'm waiting for the late bus.
Waiting for the bus in the rain."

"That's great!" I said, and I meant it.

Nan looked proud.

"What about your songs?" asked Raymond politely.

I reached for my guitar and I strummed a chord. I'd
tuned it carefully before dinner. "My singing is no good. I
can't do it."

"Come on, play us something," said Nan.

I played a D minor chord, alternating with the no-name
chord. Then I sang a snatch of the street sweeper song and
two verses of the doctor song.

"Whoa," said Ray. "I heard a little Radiohead action in
there."

"It's derivative and awful," I said. "It's bad, it's bad. It's
no good."

"No, no, it's good," said Nan sympathetically.

I put the guitar down. "Eh, I can't sing, but it's fun." I
turned to Ray. "If I get Logic, will you show me some tricks?"

"Sure, anytime," he said. "I'll show you how to use pitch

correction. You can sound almost like Kanye West if you want."

"I doubt it. Boy, he's got his hands full with Kim Kardashian." I gathered the plastic trays that the sushi came in. "What about you, Nan? Do you sing?"

She held her hands up. "I only sing Beatles songs."

"Let's hear one," I said.

"Oh, I'm out of practice."

"At least do 'Blackbird,'" said Raymond.

Nan sang, "Blackbird singing in the dead of night, Take these broken wings and learn to fly." I felt a strange lump in my throat. She finished and we all sat there.

"Damn!" I said. "Really. Damn."

"That was really good, Mom," said Raymond.

Nan wiped something from her eye. "I guess we should be going," she said. "Thank you for dinner."

I shook Raymond's hand and pointed at him. "Keep going with those songs," I told him. "You've got the touch."

I SPENT THE MORNING downloading Logic from Apple, which takes a long time because there are many gigabytes of sampled instruments. I also bought the Beatles doing "Blackbird," because Nan had sung it so well and I wanted to remember how Paul McCartney did it, also some Kanye West songs and three by Radiohead. I spent two hours watching how-to videos on YouTube and ordering a manual. Logic is not self-explanatory. It's ticklish. It does unexpected things. But, as everyone on YouTube said, once you get into it, it's very powerful. Finally I created an instrumental track and set it to Steinway Hall Piano. Each note of a real Steinway is sampled, i.e., recorded, five or six or seven times at varying volumes and loaded into something called the EXS24 Sampler. I played a B flat chord with my headphones on, using the shift-lock keyboard, which allows you to play using the letter keys of the computer, and I was stunned by how big and true it sounded. I felt like Alfred Brendel playing Mussorgsky's "The Old Castle," coaxing the licorice goodness out of a vastly expensive instrument. I felt like Maurice Ravel playing "Sad Birds." But obviously I needed a real keyboard.

I went to the music department at Best Buy and stood there for a while. "Any questions at all?" said the salesman. He was a young, friendly bass player who was going to Berklee College of Music in Boston.

I said I wanted a MIDI keyboard to hook up with Logic.

"What size are you thinking?"

"I guess the traditional eighty-eight keys, because that's the number I'm used to."

He showed me some eighty-eight-key MIDI keyboards. They cost a fortune.

"Thanks, let me study these," I said. Two children were plinking loudly and tunelessly on some portable clavichords in a different aisle. Eventually the noise began to get to me, and I went into a small glass-walled room filled with drum sets and maracas where it was quiet. Did I want to spend a vast sum for a full eighty-eight-key keyboard, a real piano-size keyboard, or did I want to get something smaller and less expensive? I decided I didn't need all eighty-eight keys, because honestly I never liked the very low and very high notes on the piano anyway—both extremes are harsh in different ways. I walked back out into the noise.

"On second thought, I think I want something more compact," I said. The salesman tapped on a box that held the Axiom forty-nine-key keyboard. "I have an Axiom 61 and I love it," he said. "It's a real workhorse. The classes at Berklee use the Axiom 49 and they've never had any problems."

So I bought it. I also bought a big book of Prince songs. I almost bought a Blue microphone as well, which had a lovely retro design. It was on display under glass near the cash register, but I restrained myself. The keyboard was enough for now. It had "aftertouch," something that real wooden pianos don't have. After you play a note, if you press down harder on the key it will detect your increased finger pressure. The keyboard was a hundred times less expensive than a Steinway Hall piano, and it was made of plastic, but it had aftertouch.

HEY THERE, PEOPLE, and welcome. This is the Poetry Pebble Tumble, and I'm your host, Paul. Tonight we convene by the light of a small, very round moon that has things to tell us, with a star near it like a pasted-on beauty mark.

I'm smoking a limited-edition Viaje Summerfest cigar.

Wow, is it strong. Strong and full of brown tuneful certainty. It's sold with loose weedy leaves poking out the end, which makes it seem exotic until you wrench them off with a turn of the wrist and roast the tip. It's my ganja. Here's to you, Bob Marley, you reconciler of opposites, you peacemaker. "One love." You said it all in a single phrase.

I'm totally stoned on this Viaje cigar. Man! Why do people need medical marijuana when there are these tightly wrapped cylinders of bliss from Latin America? I could get high thinking about the word "intrinsic."

Once in music school I was out in a Frisbee field with two friends, a clarinet player and a bassoonist. I was starting to be full of the desire to write poems, and I thought real poets talked about words all the time, so I asked a pretentious question, as poets are permitted to do. I said: Offhand, what's your favorite word? The clarinetist said, I don't know, what's yours?

"Inscrutable," I said. I gave it a big throat-wiggle of inscrutability when I said it. My two friends said, No, "inscrutable" is not that great. I was stung by their dismissal, but I didn't say so, and when my friend the bassoonist said that "cash" was his favorite word, I said, Oh yeah, cash, legal tender is the night, baby. And when the clarinet player said "kegger," I said, Oh yeah, "kegger," that's very good. I'm not going to be a naysayer of other people's pet words. That's not my role. Plus "inscrutable" isn't as good as their two. It would be nice to record the particular clunk that a Frisbee makes when it angles hard into the grass and use it in a rhythm track. Prince uses those great damped piano thumps in "Let's Go Crazy."

My role is to be here in the side yard when the moon is swimming in the deep end of the sky with the treeshapes near it. It's a full twelve feet deep under the nightpool and there's a moon ring down there, and I'm swimming down toward it and I hear the high vacuumacious sound in my eardrums and I feel the tautness pulling between my toes and I'm thankful that all my thoughts are nonsexual, and that I can sit here with my mouth open and my eyes slitted.

There are only so many nights like this. The middle of summertime, and even though it's late, a cricket like a bartender with a rag in his hand is mopping the surfaces of sound. Just one. The rest of the crickets are silent. Their abdomens are sore and chafed and they don't want to chirp anymore, they want to rest. As do I. Even this one that I'm listening to is getting drowsy. He goes: *chert chert chert*. And then there's a long pause while he sits and lets things droop, wondering if anyone's listening. And then *chert chert chert chert chert*. And then another long pause. Birds by day, crickets by night, singing away.

I'm staring right at the fucking moon and I don't care who knows it. I've heard so many different Logic sounds come from my computer and through my headphones I almost can't stand it. I'm drunk with sound, like the thirteen-year-old Brazilian girl. If I want to write something with marimba I can have marimba. If I want Balinese gamelan there's gamelan. Chinese guzheng zither? It's there. Japanese shakuhachi flute? Sure. There are innumerable kick drums, some real and some synthesized, and as for electric guitar— I've got Twangy Guitar, and New Surf Lead Guitar, and Nice Crunch Guitar, and Dirty Rotor Guitar, and dozens of others. Too much, almost. Everything's beautifully sampled. Debussy would have gone batshit if he'd had Logic on his computer. The history of music would have been completely different.

Fourteen

I NEED A MICROPHONE, THOUGH. I need a really good
stereo microphone. I spent an hour this morning reading
about microphones and hunting around on the B&H website.
B&H is an electronics store in New York where expensive
purchases scoot around in plastic bins on rollers over your
head. I bought a camcorder there once. It's run by Hasidic
Jews with hats who know everything. The prices are cheaper
on Amazon than at B&H, but that's because Amazon is using
its stock price to take over all of retailing and bankrupt the
world.

I'm not sure whether I want to get two monophonic
hundred-dollar Studio Projects B1 microphones, one for the
right track and one for the left, each of which would float in a
rubber spiderweb shockmount on a tandem microphone rack,
powered by phantom power from a Saffire 6 USB interface,
or whether I want a single shotgun stereo microphone by

Audio-Technica that was developed for broadcasters to cover the Olympics. The Audio-Technica shotgun costs about seven hundred dollars, which is obscene, but once you enter the B&H world of microphones, it seems like a reasonable price.

"You float like a feather," sings Radiohead, "In a beautiful world." I've listened several times to the Radiohead songs, because it was nice of Raymond to say he heard a bit of them in what I sang. I'm not sure I hear it myself, but I was pleased and touched. Sometimes that's what you need, just a quick, casual word of knowledgeable encouragement. Radiohead reminds me a little of the songs in the *Garden State* soundtrack. Now, that's a soundtrack. They were all just songs that Zach Braff liked, so he put them in his movie. And there's that beautiful moment near the beginning where Natalie Portman hands him the headphones and she watches him listen to the song and she smiles her huge, innocent Natalie Portman smile.

If you're a woman and you want to make it in movies, that's what you need: an enormous mouth. Because you're talking. Somewhere above you is a big, sensitive microphone on a boom pole that is listening to what you say. You have to have a really big stretchy Carly Simon mouth with big lips that want to be open all the time. And you want to have teeth that go on forever. You don't just have bicuspids, you have tricuspids and quadricuspids. Look at Julia Roberts or Gwyneth Paltrow. The men, too. Tom Cruise, huge mouth. Fred Astaire, Bing Crosby, Sinatra—all bigmouthed men.

Brad Pitt, fairly big mouth. You don't need to be tall. Natalie Portman is tiny. When she became the black swan she was so terribly thin I worried about her. Her mouth was bigger than ever. And lately, in *No Strings Attached*, she's still beautiful but her hair looks tired and she's perhaps wearing too much eye makeup. Her great moment was when she handed over the headphones and smiled in *Garden State*.

The bad guys in movies have small mouths. Good poets often have small mouths, too, whereas good singers have big mouths. Think of Whitney Houston: small face, big mouth. Good poets often have beards, which make their mouths exceedingly small, sometimes invisible. Robert Browning had a very tiny mouth, I think. Stanley Kunitz, medium-size mouth. It's a completely different approach to utterance. Maybe that's the fundamental difference. I have a small mouth, and it's slightly asymmetrical. Even before I smoked a cigar I talked like a cigar smoker.

What a disgusting habit. I love it.

I'VE BEEN READING UP on anemia. I was surprised to learn that blackstrap molasses has more iron than anything except meat—much more iron than collards. Spinach is nothing, forget spinach. Roz doesn't eat meat.

I watched some Logic tutorials by Matt Shadetek, who teaches at a music school in Manhattan called Dubspot, and I learned how to use the chord memorizer. The chord memorizer allows you to play any sort of chord you want by playing a single key, even chords that are so widely spaced that a single pianist couldn't play them. I layered some impressionistic sounds and loaded them in the chord memorizer and recorded a little piece. When I listened to it I realized that the harmony sounded alarmingly like Debussy's "Sunken Cathedral." I guess that's not too surprising, since it's my favorite piece of music. On top of it, into the computer's tinny microphone, I sang, "Only evil can come of evil. Only evil can come of evil. Only evil can come of evil. Drown it with good."

My voice was small and scratchy. I like the idea of having a scratchy voice.

Time to take the dog for a walk.

AT FRESH MARKET I bought a jar of pesto, a shrink-wrapped hunk of Parmesan cheese, and a blue box of cellentani pasta—the spiral kind that holds the pesto best. I thought of writing a dance song in which there would be a sudden silence and then a low voice, like the voice in "Low Rider," would intone the names of kinds of pasta. "Penne rigate, bum bum bum bum—rigatoni. Penne rigate, bum bum bum bum—rigatoni." Then: "Cellentani! Cellentani! Cellentani!" I paused in the bulk-food aisle, looking at the plastic canisters of sesame seeds and poppy seeds, and I thought of Roz wanting to eat the sidewalk. I bought a big jug of Brer Rabbit blackstrap molasses, which is in the baking aisle. On the way home I listened to part of a *Sodajerker* podcast interview with Jimmy Webb, who wrote "Someone Left the Cake Out in the Rain," and then I sent Roz a text: "The internet says that blackstrap molasses contains more iron than the Lusitania. I bought a jug of it for you in case you need it. I can drop it by anytime if you're feeling anemic. Love P"

She wrote back, "Thanks, that's good to know."

Why is it that certain timbres of speaking voice are pleasing and others aren't? Think of Bob Edwards. He was fired from NPR. Why? We don't know. "Hi, I'm Bob Edwards and this is *Morning Edition*." Every day we were there with the radio on, listening with our coffee and our bagel. It was a glorious thing to listen to Bob Edwards on *Morning Edition*, because he had a little bit of pain and suffering in his voice. There were nicks and dings on his vocal cords. They met and vibrated and did what they needed to do to get the sound of his words out, but they were slightly damaged, and the damage made for interesting whispery overtones. His voice wasn't as damaged as Melanie's, who did the roller-skate song. Not as damaged as Meatloaf's. But it was definitely timeworn, and we loved that.

Bob Edwards talked into a big, expensive studio microphone, and here's the scandal. His microphone, like most in the talk radio business, like most in the music recording business, was a monophonic microphone.

Monophonic sound. What a vile and diseased thing. I've got "mono" voice. Mono! No, we don't want that. We want it in stereo, obviously. For at least forty years we've wanted it in stereo. Ever since I was a kid we've wanted it in stereo. Don't tell me that you're recording voices in mono. That's just plain awful. That's criminal. And yet the sound engineers persist. The singer sings her lungs out and she listens to the take and she wonders why her big chorus sounds so thin on tape when she knows it sounded so full and phat when she sang it. Well, it's obvious. She sounds thin because she's singing into a very fancy, very expensive, very mono microphone. She says, "Phil, can you beef up the sound a little?" So the sound engineer does his usual tricks—he doubles the vocals, or he adds some reverb, or he cranks up the compression. Maybe he runs it through a special filter called an exciter that adds some glitter to the upper end. But he can't change the fundamental fact that he's manipulating a mono signal.

I ordered the seven-hundred-dollar stereo shotgun from B&H. It's time to get serious.

Fifteen

THIS IS WHAT I MEAN. The experts do not know what they're talking about. They say we should eat margarine, not butter, and that if you can pinch an inch of your husband's arm, chances are he's too fat. And then they say margarine's bad because it's full of trans fat. They say drinking destroys brain cells, and then that turns out to be totally bogus, based on no research, and we're supposed to have two drinks a day. They say spinach is full of iron, when really they should be talking about molasses. Same with the singing voice. They record the vox humana as vox humono because it's always been done that way. It allows them to place the voice at dead center in the stereo space. If the lead singer sways from side to side, carried away by the beat, the sound stands still. That's very convenient, but it's wrong. Of all sounds, the human voice is the sound that we hear best, just as faces are the sights we see best. The slight skeptical contraction at the corners of the eyes, the tiny, indulgent almost smile—we're immediately aware of those clues, because we're born experts at reading faces. And likewise we hear a hundred subtle clues in a singing voice, clues about love and regret and rapture, and some of those clues are dulled or lost in mono.

Stereo recording was the biggest revelation of my life, bigger than any poem. Listening to our mono record player was pleasant, but everything was tinny and far away. When I was six I had a record of Prokofiev's *Peter and the Wolf*—the part of the grandfather is played by the bassoon—and a record of Brazilian drumming called *Batucada Fantástica*, and I played my father's copy of Bach's *Art of the Fugue*. I was taking piano lessons by then, and I was fascinated by the idea of inverting a melody, making the notes go down when they originally went up, and up when they originally went down. Then the craziness hit. The Beatles hit, and Leonard Bernstein hit, and *2001: A Space Odyssey* used Strauss's *Zarathustra*, and my father subscribed to *Stereo Review*, and I began drumming *Batucada Fantástica* rhythms on a large cardboard tube. One summer we got a set of Bose 501 speakers and a minimalist AR turntable with a visible rubber band that turned the platter—AR stood for Acoustic Research—and a Yamaha stereo receiver, and a set of white JVC headphones. Both earpieces had volume dials, so that you could crank the volume up or down on each side. I put the headphones on, and I lowered the needle on Zubin Mehta conducting *The Rite of Spring*, and suddenly I was there, enclosed in the oxygenated spatial spread of stereophonic sound. I was there with the panicked piccolo, and the bass clarinet was a few feet away, and the timpani surged over to the left, mallets going so fast you couldn't see them. I couldn't believe how big a world it was—how much bigger and better stereo was than mono. The human ear had figured out something many eons ago, millions of years ago, in the sacred springtime of the world, long before there were humans, in fact—something basic that very smart scientists took a while to figure out: You need two ears. You need to sample how a sound changes when you move your head slightly. If you move your head, then you can determine what's behind you and what's in front of you. You hear a cracking twig somewhere off to the far right. Something's out there. Is it a barking deer? No, it's Igor Stravinsky, giving us the super-high-pitched bassoon solo that begins the convulsion.

THE RITE OF SPRING caused problems for Debussy. It blew him out of the water. It frightened him. It made him feel old. It used motifs and harmonic innovations that Debussy had first used in "Nuages," but it went much further with them. There's a photo of Debussy and Stravinsky side by side in Debussy's apartment. I assume they've just played the four-hand piano reduction of *The Rite of Spring* together. Debussy, standing, looks thoughtful, perhaps tired. He's sinking. He knows he's got cancer. He's been taking morphine and cocaine. Hokusai's wave is hanging on the wall behind him. Stravinsky looks arrogant and cocky. Stravinsky was, in fact, arrogant and cocky. He was a cold man. He was not nice to his children. Robert Craft wrote that he was surprised, years later, when Stravinsky clanged on a wineglass with his knife to summon a waiter.

For a while, everything Stravinsky did, he did with Debussy in mind. I think that's why he chose the bassoon to play the solo that begins *The Rite of Spring*. It's a simple pagan melody—you can play it all on the white keys of the piano—and the logical instrument to play it would be a flute. Ah, but he couldn't: Debussy had already created a sensation with *Afternoon of a Faun*, inspired by Mallarmé's frisky erotic poem, which begins with—what instrument of the orchestra? Anyone. A solo flute, exactly. Debussy's flute was a lithe, twisty, innocently suggestive danseuse, who went here and there, through some sharps and flats, showing a bit of leotard, and then the orchestra came in to help out, and then the solo flute returned. Stravinsky's beginning was a sort of ironic commentary on Debussy's flute. He knew the bassoon could do it—he'd already had a success with the huge bassoon solo in *The Firebird Suite*, which is a berceuse, a lullaby: a very simple solo in the mid-range of the bassoon that begins on a B flat and goes no higher than a high F. I played it once with a youth orchestra, doing my best to sound like Bernie Garfield in Philadelphia. It's warm and loving and faintly exotic and soft-feathered over the violas, and then the whole orchestra comes in with a chord that's impossibly lush and chromatic, chromaticism that Liszt, Chopin, Mussorgsky, and Scriabin might have come up with if they'd all been locked in a water closet together for several days, and then he goes back to Firebirding sadly and plainly with the bassoon. That's the way the Russians would do it. Rimsky-Korsakov would have done it that way. The bassoon is mother Russia, souped up for export to Paris.

But at the same time as he was writing *Firebird*, Stravinsky was working on *The Rite of Spring*. And he thought, Here's what I'm going to do this time. This'll really get the Frenchies. I'm going to take the whole nineteenth century and all of its comfortable clubby conveniences—its umbrellas, its empire wainscoting, its pigeonhole desks, its velvet cases of surgical tools, its reassuringly civilized chamber concerts—and I'm going to use the bassoon with its keys and its pads and its maplewood smoothness to sum all that up, but then I'm going to torture it. I'm going to pitch it up high where the flute normally plays. I'm going to make the music strain to achieve its innocence. I'm going to start on a high C, way up in the impossible uppermost register of the bassoon, and then I'll take it even higher and ask for a high D. It'll almost sound like a flute—Rimsky-Korsakov had said in his book on orchestration that the high bassoon can sound rather like a flute, and it does—but it won't be a flute, it'll be the agonized first-desk bassoonist, who must struggle with every tendon showing in his neck to reach that high D, leaking air around the reed, ignoring the patronizing backward glances from the cellos. Debussy knew what was going on. He knew that *The Rite of Spring* was in some ways a direct attack on his and

Mallarmé's flora-and-faunish pan-pipingly impressionistic idea of springtime. He wrote a letter to somebody after he'd played the piano-four-hands version with Stravinsky and said he was disturbed at its violence. Debussy must have sensed what was happening and been irritated by it, as well as jealous: the falling chromaticism of his gentle flute solo replaced by this sweating, straining mop-headed bassoonist who leads the way for the sonic pandemic to follow. Just to make the connection perfectly clear, Stravinsky uses a flute to play part of the melody once. And then he returns to the bassoon to reprise it, half a step lower. It's even harder to play shifted down a half step.

This is what *The Rite of Spring* is all about. It's an act of ambitious aggression, a mockery of chromaticism—it's chromaticism taken to the point of pure polytonality—and he's forcing us, the backward bassoonists, to lead the charge. And we love it because we get so few solos. Almost never do we get to start a huge orchestra going. But here we do. We're grateful. The solo is still in my fingers. When I sing it to myself my fingers make the old motions.

THERE'S ANOTHER GOOD REASON why Stravinsky chose the bassoon and not the flute. I understood this only later, when I'd begun making my own reeds. He couldn't begin the *Rite* with a flute because a flute is a tube of metal with a metal blowhole. It isn't biological. It's something melted and smelted. What he wanted was the squirming, elemental, tropical, green-fused growth-urge of Spring: he wanted cane plants, *Arundo donax*, sprouting an inch a day out of wet soil, hacked down by migrant farmers in Arles, dried and soaked, dried and soaked, fashioned with a bit of wire and some thread into a primitive croaking thing, a double reed, and stuck on the end of a breathing tube whose keys were veins, not levers, like something out of H. R. Giger's bio-machine interiors for *Alien*. The bassoon solo is a joule of sunlight hitting the cane marsh. Grubs and aphids stir cuntily in the bass clarinet. Night soil decays into a broth of fetid but nutritious water and is pumped high in the xylem vessels. Virgins in muddy ballet shoes press Miracle-Gro tablets into the roots of the chosen canes. The bassoonists murmur their prices to the cane dealers. Norman Herzberg and Maurice Allard, representing the German and French designs of bassoon, respectively, do a grunting dance, jabbing ceremonially with their files and gougers. It's all there. It's all about the bassoon.

And I never got to play *The Rite of Spring*. I regret that. I listened to it pump forth from the Bose speakers, and I practiced it in practice rooms, imagining the rest of the orchestra, and I played *The Firebird Suite* and even performed one of Stravinsky's later pieces, his *Symphonies of Wind Instruments*, which has a difficult patch of low-register bassoonery. But never the *Rite*.

Sixteen

I CALLED ROZ UP and I asked her how she was doing.

"At the moment, not great," she said. "I'm having one of my epic bloodlettings. It's not as bad as last month, though."

"That's good, at least. Maybe the worst is over."

"I doubt it. I've got something important I want to talk to you about. But not right now. Peter Breggin is here to give an interview about psychotropic drugs and murder."

"Sounds provocative." I knew what she was going to tell me—that she was engaged to Harris the doctor. Fuck that!

I'm eating a peanut butter cracker right now. These little round snacks are my mainstays sometimes. I'm up in the barn. I'm beginning to get a studio arranged. I've got a folding table, and my speakers, and my keyboard, and my guitar, and my guitar pick, and my new microphone pointing directly at my mouth, which is full of cracker. Electricity comes in via an orange extension cord I've run up through a hole in the floor. It's not too hot yet. I've got my dirty flip-flops on, and my dark green vat-dyed T-shirt, and I need a serious haircut and I look like a Gerry Rafferty back from the dead. Remember "Baker Street," with the gigantic sax solo that single-handedly brought saxophone session players out from dark corners where they'd been hiding, begging for pennies? When I landed in the USA, home from Paris and full of Rimbaud and Mallarmé, Gerry Rafferty was singing, "This city desert makes you feel so cold, it's got so many people, but it's got no soul." Everything lay before me.

Let me just take another bite of cracker. Dang, that's good. Each molar-crushing expression of taste has more to offer, till finally you're down to the dry crumbly nubblies that pack themselves into the crevices of your molars. If I were writing a poem I'd worry about the fact that I'd just used "molar" twice in a sentence. But I'm not writing a poem, because right now I'm getting ready to write songs, baby. My fingers and toes feel ready.

I've published three books of poems and an anthology. That's plenty. Nobody wants to read more than three books of poems by anyone. You see these poets who are up to seven, eight, nine books, ten, *eleven* books of poems. It's grotesque. They should have stopped at four.

OKAY, I just spent all day doing music. I worked through a chapter of the official Logic manual, which is 504 pages long, learning how to think like a producer and politely prune away some distracting Moog synthesizer chirpings from a song that came in a DVD in the back of the book. Then I spent an hour recording random percussion sounds from around the house. The empty guitar box made a kick drump thump. The top of a rusty can of anti-mildew paint made a sort of panting, brush-on-cymbal sound when I moved my finger over it. The pasta pot, filled with half an inch of water, produced a spacey warped noise—I've always liked the way it distorts the sloshings of water as I wash it. Slosh wash. With my fingernail I plinked a china bowl that Roz gave me. I banged the broom handle on the floor and got another kind of kick drum. Then I had an inspiration, and I got out the egg slicer from under the kitchen counter. I wanted to make a song of the egg slicer. I plucked the wires. There were four notes that were surprisingly close to a minor scale. I sliced the egg slicer samples in Logic and figured out how to use the fade tool to get rid of the little pops where I'd made the cuts.

I recorded some harmony, using the Steinway Hall Piano—I always seem to go back to the Steinway—then added several jingly, tinkly rhythms from the Indian and Middle Eastern drum kit, and some guitar, and then experimented with some sampled classical male voices singing "ah" and "oh," and placed the egg-slicer sounds on top. I guess I was making some kind of sound salad. But the egg slicer didn't fit well and I muted it. The broom was pretty good, it had a sort of double thump, but the egg slicer was a disappointment. I couldn't find any handclap samples anywhere in Logic—although I'm sure they're there somewhere—so I recorded some of my own, and I watched a YouTube video on how to take a single, inadequate handclap and double it and then shift the claps around so that they sound realer, moving one clap track to the left and one to the right of the stereo center. But the handclaps sounded corny and I cut them out.

I played what I had so far, and thought I had the beginnings of a song. All it needed was the melody and the words. I set up a "Male Ambient Lead" vocal track. My underpowered voice became enormous in my headphones. I started singing along to the loop with my huge stereo voice. At first I sang wordlessly: ba-doodle doodle doodle doo, doot doodle doo. Then I sang, "Waiting for the time to come, waiting for the time to come, waiting for the time to come." There it was, the beginning of a song, and it had only taken me four hours. Four hours of sweating in the ridiculously hot barn.

I went into the house and had some iced coffee and checked email. Tim had gotten arrested again in Syracuse at a drone protest outside Hancock Field, along with five other people. He sent me the link to a short video about the protest, and a link to the antiwar song by Eric Bogle, "No Man's Land," aka "Green Fields of France," as performed by the kid in his dorm room. The kid's YouTube name was Kirobaito. It's just him and his guitar and a webcam. He's got a flag of Scotland hung on the wall behind him. At one point his roommates try to distract him, he explains in the notes to the video, but he keeps singing, acknowledging them with a tiny smile. His computer screen is reflected in his glasses. The song is addressed to a nineteen-year-old boy named Willie McBride, who died in France in World War I. I thought I'd just watch a little, just enough to thank Tim for the video. But it was so good I kept going. "A whole generation was butchered and damned," Kirobaito sang. "The suffering the sorrow the glory the shame / The killing the dying was all done in vain." It ended. I watched it again. I read some of the comments. "Well done dude." "Woah. That was beautiful." "Listened to this on repeat for at least an hour now. This is awesome." When it ended for the second time, I said, "These fucking stupid wars!" to the empty kitchen. I wrote Tim to thank him. "Tim, you were right—I'm crying. Thank you for telling me about this song. And thank you for going to Syracuse."

I WATCHED SOME MORE VIDEOS of antiwar demonstrations, including one in which a policeman goes methodically down a line of seated protesters, squirting pepper spray in their eyes. I looked up the First Amendment to the Constitution and wrote a tune for some words taken from it:

> Peaceably
> To assemble
> To petition
> For redress

Maybe, with practice, my singing will improve. I practiced the bassoon for years until I sounded decent. But singing is more fundamental. You either can or you can't. "Nice pipes, Tamika," as Jack Black says in *School of Rock*.

I spent half an hour at Planet Fitness, and afterward I sat in the car and pressed the space bar to listen to bits of the songs I'd made. It occurred to me that the words—"Waiting for the time to come"—were perhaps uncomfortably close to John Mayer's song "Waiting on the World to Change." I have that song. I plugged my headphones into my iPhone and listened to it while I drove home. The funny thing is, Roz and I once had a minor difference of opinion about Mayer's song, back when it was being played a lot. Her point was that you can't just wait. You can't just say, in a sort of smug way, We're the new generation and there's nothing we can do now, but when we come to power everything will be different and the soldiers will be home for Christmas and there won't be yellow ribbons out. You have to object to the wrong right now, even though you're at a distance from the action, and even though your elders are in power. Roz was right, of course, but on the other hand, Mayer's song was at least the registering of a dissatisfaction. It's true that he was saying that we should simply acquiesce for the time being, but patience can be a virtue, and he had a nice voice and it was a good song and I liked it. Turns out Mayer went to Berklee College of Music. Roz loved his song "Your Body Is a Wonderland." That's a Tyrconnell song.

I touched the little atomic genius sign to hear more songs

like Mayer's "Waiting," and "Caring Is Creepy" came on, from the *Garden State* soundtrack. I skipped it, and I also skipped a nice remix by Nosaj Thing called "Islands," and I skipped the Weepies doing "World Spins Madly On" because I'd heard it recently, and then I listened to part of Paul Simon doing "Slip Slidin' Away"—Paul Simon never pushes his beautiful voice, and come to think of it, he's got a small mouth. Small mouth, big songs. There are always exceptions. One Paul Simon album was so big and so controversial that it helped end the apartheid government in South Africa. And then I came to Tracy Chapman singing "Change." I listened to the whole thing, really took in the words for the first time.

Tracy Chapman can sing. There's a pent strength of held-back fast vibrato in her voice sometimes, at big moments, and then other times she just lets the notes slide out unobstructed. "If everything you think you know / Makes your life unbearable / Would you change?" Who knew that "know" and "unbearable" could rhyme? But they do. The music makes them rhyme.

And then John Lennon's "Watching the Wheels" came on and I couldn't listen to John because I was so completely destroyed by Tracy Chapman. I wasn't ready for John right then. I wasn't prepared for him.

Tomorrow I'm flying to Chicago to be on a panel about the future of poetry. I'm a mobile music-maker now: I've bought a small, twenty-five-key keyboard with keys that are slightly smaller than normal, like Schroeder's piano. It fits in my briefcase.

Seventeen

I WOKE UP VERY EARLY, before it was light, and by the glow of my phone I read a little of Pat Pattison's ebook on how to write better song lyrics. Pat Pattison teaches at Berklee. One of his students was John Mayer, he is at pains to let us know. At the beginning of his book he thanks Mayer and some of his fellow students "for showing how well all this stuff can work." Pattison is not a humble man. The mother-of-pearl shell-diving exercise in his first chapter, he says, has over the years "proved to be a mainstay for many successful songwriters, including Grammy winners John Mayer and Gillian Welch."

Here's how you do the diving exercise, according to Pat Pattison. You imagine a random object—anything at all, could be a back porch or a puddle—and you dive toward it. You try to understand how it affects all seven of your senses, including your organic sense and your kinesthetic sense. You set a timer and do this for ten minutes first thing in the morning. You take notes. By the sixth minute, things really get going, Pattison says. You're on your way down, "diving, plunging, heading for the soft pink and blue glow." Then, ding, time's up.

That sounded pretty good. I tried it in bed. I started the iPhone timer and began typing notes. What was I diving for? I didn't want to think about a back porch or a puddle. I was diving down to reach the drain at the swimming pool at summer camp. The drain under the diving boards was twelve feet deep, I knew that. I had tried before and hadn't been able to do it, but now it was toward the end of camp, and my swimming had gotten stronger. It was a YMCA day camp, and there were swimming certificates. They gave you little cards when you'd progressed to a certain level. This was when I was eight or nine. I'd gotten a Guppy card, and a Minnow card—I was nowhere near a Flying Fish or a Shark—and I took a huge gulp of air and surface-dived toward the drain. I struggled down, kicking so hard my body twisted in the water, till the drain began to come into focus. It was round and black and had a number of large holes in it. I thought I wasn't going to be able to reach it. I saw—

And then my alarm timer went off, playing its loud marimba tune, with a final plink of syncopation. I turned it off. I reset it for another ten minutes. What I saw on the drain was a pale pink piece of chewing gum, the very same piece of pink baby-Jesus gum I'd seen at the drinking fountain at school. I didn't touch it. I touched the terrifying drain itself. I looked up and saw somebody's legs hit the water a mile above me. I pushed off from the bottom and clawed to the surface. I didn't tell anyone I'd touched the drain that day, but I had.

Four or five years later, my grandparents took us on a cruise. It was a Swan Hellenic Cruise, with a full complement of tanned, elderly, witty classicists from Oxford who gave lectures on-site at Paestum and Pompeii and at the rebuilt ruins of the palace at Knossos. I took a picture of a black cat near one of the columns of the Parthenon that had been reassembled after the Turks stored ammunition there and it blew up. One of the professors, J. V. Luce, had a theory that Plato's Atlantis was actually Minoan Crete, which had suffered a terrible tidal wave when a nearby island volcano blew and then sank into the sea, forming a caldera. Professor Luce said that there was a core of truth to the Atlantis story, that the sinking island and the tidal destruction of the center of Minoan civilization had merged, and that Plato had gotten the dimensions of Atlantis wrong by a simple factor of ten, which was an easy thing to do because of the cumbersome way in which numbers were notated at the time. I was tremendously excited by this theory. It was definitely true, no question.

The timer's marimba went off again and I didn't bother to reset it. There was, I recall, a beautiful long empty beach on Crete with a rusty wrecked ship on its side a few hundred feet from shore. I swam out to it with my new facemask on and saw the ribs of the wreck through the bright blue water. It was entirely covered with pale yellow seaweeds about the size of Lay's potato chips that moved gently in the currents. I felt a fear of the empty blue water and the yellow weedy wreck and I swam back to shore.

And then we went to a small island—I think it was Mykonos—with many white houses on steep streets that led down to the water. "You need some fins," my grandmother said. She went into a tourist shop and bought me a pair of black swim fins and a snorkel. The fins were difficult to walk in, but they propelled you through the water with remarkable speed. The beach was in a cove, with high rocks around, and I swam out to the deepest part, breathing through my gurgly new snorkel. It had little rubber flanges you could bite on to hold it in your mouth. I stared down at the green-black weeds and the lumpy rocks. I sucked in air and upended myself and dove, and I got about halfway down and then turned back. The water was deeper than the YMCA pool. It was darker, too. The light angled into it like light coming through venetian blinds. I thought I saw something moving down there, something oddly furry, like a hedgehog. Perhaps it was a sea cucumber. I took a breath and bit down on the now useless snorkel and began my descent, trying to swim like the scuba people in *Voyage to the Bottom of the Sea*, with my arms at my sides.

The fins helped me go deep fast. The facemask pushed hard against my upper lip and around my eyes. I kept going. And then the daylight dimmed and I felt currents of cold water touching me like arms.

I reached out toward the mysterious woolly sea cucumber,

if that's what it was, but there were black seaweeds all around it and my fear was growing. I saw a spiny sea urchin next to it. I thought, I'm in an element that doesn't want me here. Don't go this deep. I turned and kicked my fins and swam upward. I flailed through into air and light and breathed.

So that is what Pat Pattison helped me remember. Is there a song in all that? I don't think so. Maybe if I were John Mayer there would be, or Gillian Welch. Who is Gillian Welch? I'll have to check her out.

Eighteen

I'LL TELL YOU ONE THING. Two things. First, I like wind. It blows things around and it blows the cigar smoke away. I've only smoked about half of an Arturo Fuente Gran Reserva and I'm already feeling subjected to an unusual force of gravity. The world has gotten larger and more massive, with more liquefied rock in it, and it's pulling me down toward its center, into the car seat, where I'm sitting. The second thing is, when you smoke a big, bad cigar first thing in the morning, it makes you need to go to the bathroom. You'd better be at home or parked near a bathroom when you smoke that cigar. It's almost uncontrollable.

I'm back from the Chicago gig. They gave me a gorgeous blue check for a thousand dollars. I stayed in the guest room of an English professor and his charming and funny wife who had not dyed her hair. I always like women who don't dye their hair. The guest room was in the attic and I had my own bathroom. Before the event I lay on the bed moaning, "Why am I here?" and trying to figure out what to say about the future of poetry, and then I "boweled down," as Roz used to say. Of course the toilet clogged. It was inevitable. I flushed a few times with no results and then the chain broke. Shit. You know the scene in *Anger Management* when John Turturro says, "I took a dump on his porch"? That's what I thought of. I felt no anger, though, only fatalistic acceptance. The professor was out meeting another panelist at the airport and I didn't want to ask the charming, funny woman for a plunger. I took the back lid off, taking care not to clank it, and tinkered in the tank for a while, and then I took a rash chance and forced it to flush manually by lifting the slimy rubber stopper. Miraculously, the toilet conceded. What a beautiful sight to see that horrorshow of embarrassment swirl away. I put on my lucky tie—it's one of my father's narrow paisley ties.

At the symposium the consensus was that poetry had a rosy future. Lots of interesting work was being done in out-of-the-way places like Stockton, California, and new means of distribution were bringing imaginary gardens with real toads in them to poem-starved folk in the hinterlands and innerlands who'd never heard of Marianne Moore. I said how much I liked getting a poem of the day by email from the Poetry Foundation and that I'd rediscovered Thomas Hardy that way. There was a young panelist from Harvard named Somebody Abel who made the point that we think that people were reading poetry aloud to each other every evening by the fireside a hundred years ago, reciting Tennyson for giggles, and it simply isn't true. He read from a piece written by George Gissing in which Gissing said that in his experience among common folk nobody had the slightest interest in or reverence for poetry and nobody knew a line of it. Abel said it's always been that way and it always will be that way and the whole push to teach the Great Books is just a way of making students miserable. I thought that was refreshing, but another panelist got huffy. Afterward we all went out for a long dinner with some MFA students at a noisy "bistro" where we had to shout and scream and sample fancy wines while all the while pretending we were talking in normal voices. I was somewhat tipsy and wiped out when we got back, and I went to sleep and had a nightmare about having to serve slices of cold brain to rich people in a black-and-white movie, and I woke up at three a.m. I wrote Roz a note on a postcard of the Sears Tower, now called the Willis Tower: "Newscrawl, five Chicago panelists agree American poetry has a future. I miss your delightful scarved self. -P." I still couldn't sleep, so I pulled out my new twenty-five-key keyboard and hooked it up to my computer and made a song fragment called "Marry Me," using the computer's tinny microphone. I think maybe it's the best thing I've done so far. The end goes:

> There's lots to do
> Plenty to see
> And that's why you
> Should get married to me

In the morning, when the charming wife was gone, I told the professor that the attic toilet had gone *hors de service*, but that I thought I'd fixed it. He said, "Oh, I'm so sorry, yes, that toilet is very delicate."

An MFA student, a poet, had been assigned the job of driving me to the airport. She played me her favorite song, which was a live performance of "In the Gloaming," done by Jonatha Brooke in a cappella harmony with another woman. "Will you think of me and love me," Jonatha Brooke sings, "As you did once long ago?" The MFA student and I drove up the ramp to the airport drop-off doing our best not to cry our eyes out. She closed the trunk and I thanked her and flew home.

I'VE FINISHED SEASON TWO of *Downton Abbey* and burned out on episodes of *The Office*—Dwight is simply intolerable. Instead today I watched a little of John Cusack's movie *War, Inc.*, and then I watched him and Minnie Driver in *Grosse Pointe Blank*. Minnie Driver plays a woman with a radio show in Grosse Pointe, Michigan, and John Cusack plays a disillusioned hit man, formerly employed by the CIA.

People believe that the CIA is forever—that it's an immovable fixture of American government, like Congress or the Supreme Court—but it was begun with an executive order by a president and it could be ended just as easily. It exists by presidential whim. Obama could shut it down tomorrow, but he doesn't want to. People believe wars are inevitable, that human nature can't change, but think of capital punishment. In England people were once disemboweled and castrated in front of a cheering crowd, with their heads put on spikes for viewing. In India they executed criminals by dragging them through the streets and having an elephant step on their heads. Now most countries have outlawed capital punishment. Or think of dueling. Ben Jonson killed a man in a duel. Manet dueled an art critic and wounded him with a sword. Pushkin, who fought dozens of duels, died of a bullet wound to the abdomen. Abraham Lincoln almost fought a duel. Nobody duels now. It's inconceivable. It isn't basic to anything. Centuries of patrician tradition, absurd rituals, faces slapped, gauntlets stiffly thrown, times appointed, companions holding out pistols in velvet cases in the park at dawn, the iron laws of honor—we know now it's all hokum. Progress is possible. Drones on autopilot are not inevitable.

Although she's British, Minnie Driver can do a remarkably good American accent. She's got a good ear. She can sing, too, I just found out. She's got a song about how she wants to be taken out into the deeper water. I like it and I like her big mouth and her big jaw. She's a bigmouthed babe. She had a fling with the man who starred in *The Bourne Identity*. It ended badly, as I remember. Matt Damon. He broke up with her on *Oprah*, which doesn't seem like something Jason Bourne would do. Another actress who can really sing is Scarlett Johansson. She hums and wails and whispers in a song by J. Ralph called "One Whole Hour." "I know just what it's like," she says, "to wait for a voice inside." The music makes the words fit. Did Scarlett go out with Matt Damon, too? No, but he starred with her in a family movie called *We Bought a Zoo*. No elephants step on criminals' heads in that movie. It's just not done anymore.

THE BOURNE IDENTITY has one of the best movie scores ever written. It's by John Powell, a British composer. It begins with a big bassoon solo, sailing in over a long chord in the strings. Think of that, beginning a spy movie with a bassoon. I first saw *The Bourne Identity* in a hotel room in Washington, D.C. I had just been in a march against the Iraq War, which was imminent. It's the only protest march I've ever been in. We took to the streets and we walked around neighborhoods in Washington shouting crude rhymes: "One, two, three, four, we don't want your oil war." My sign said: THIS WAR WILL DO NO GOOD. The march didn't do much good, either, unfortunately. We're still waiting on the world to change.

Roz was with me, and when we went up to the hotel room our feet hurt from marching all day. We took off our shoes and ordered a pizza and watched *The Bourne Identity* and loved it, and I thought, This is about the best movie score I've ever heard, and I want to hear it again. So I bought it. For the percussion section, Powell uses crazy camera-shutter sounds, huge flabby drums, shakers, rattling sheets of what sounds like fiberglass or plywood, and sixty-megahertz electrical feedback hums. There's a touch of *Batucada Fantástica* in it, but it's its own thing—and there's not a cheesy passage in the whole score. I'd give anything to have written that music. Composers have ripped off Powell's *Bourne* score many times since then. You'll suddenly hear it in a fight scene or a chase scene. I wonder whether Powell is upset at being strip-mined that way—maybe not. The movie score business has a low opinion of itself, and its leading lights seem unconcerned by everyone's habit of adaptive reuse. Powell worked for a while with Hans Zimmer, and Hans Zimmer is one of the biggest and cheerfullest ripper-offers of them all, to the point where the Holst Foundation brought suit against him for stealing music note for note from *The Planets*. One of Powell's colleagues in the Zimmer atelier was Harry Gregson-Williams. Listen to the *Bourne Identity* soundtrack and then watch *Déjà Vu*, with Denzel Washington—score by Harry Gregson-Williams. You'll gasp at the audacity in places. It isn't plagiarism—no spot is precisely the same—and yet it's a theft of almost everything good about Powell's score, harmonies, percussion, slow solos, mood builds. It's worse than the endless classical music recyclings by John Williams, who has rifled every late Romantic pocket, and James Horner of *Titanic* fame. And yet Powell and Gregson-Williams were colleagues and friends under Zimmer. Maybe Powell gave his permission, I don't know. I'd like to know. I think about this a lot.

Debussy was stolen from constantly during his lifetime, not just by Stravinsky but by everyone. His originality was smothered in a wave of second-tier Debussyism. It depressed him. In 1915 he told a friend that the Debussyists were killing him. No, as a matter of fact, tobacco was killing him.

Nineteen

NOW I REALLY FEEL RICH. Gene sent me an email to tell me that the University of Somewhere Far Away With a Big Football Team had ordered two hundred more copies of *Only Rhyme* for the fall term. "I thought you'd like to know," he wrote. He wants to encourage me. So much of what an editor does is encouragement, flattery, and acts of kindness. They're such good people. I've never had a bad experience with an editor. And now they must grope their way through the ebook revolution, squabbling with Amazon, trying to figure out how to make money. They believe in what they do. Some of them must have secret doubts. Another memoir this month, another set of blurbs to solicit, another mailing of bound galleys to people like me who don't read them. I have guilty stacks of them in my office, each with an enthusiastic letter tucked in the front. Wave after wave of unread words. Blah, guilt!

After I made the circuit of the upper-body machines at Planet F, I sat in the car, parked in a tiny patch of shade in back near a self-seeded oak tree, and I said aloud, "What have we given to the world?" We in the United States, I meant. What do we have to be proud of? Warfarin and Risperdal and Effexor and Abilify and Hellfire missiles and supermax prisons and the revenge killing of Osama bin Laden—and the Staple Singers. Music. I'd give anything to sing like the Staple Singers. Anything I have. "Undertaker, please drive slow." The Staple Singers is what we've given to the world.

I drove past the trendy pizza place where a girl with a beautiful mouth used to work. She rarely smiled. She just tucked in the corners of the pizza boxes and handed them over the counter to people with twenty-dollar bills. She didn't have to smile. She doesn't work there anymore, but I was shocked all over again at the memory of how lovely she was. Just a pizza girl. Now she's off somewhere, living life, paying off her college loans, giving other people the benefit of her selfless amazing mouth.

Today I watched *Coal Miner's Daughter*, with Sissy Spacek. See what I mean? Small actress, big mouth. What stunned me about the movie is that Sissy Spacek, whom I've never understood before because she has such a tiny nose, did all the singing in the movie. None of it was overdubbed by Loretta Lynn. It's all Spacek's own singing. She spent days and days with Loretta Lynn—a year together, said Loretta in the bonus video—practicing Loretta's songs. Loretta taught

Sissy all her nuances and tricks. She, Loretta, said she can't watch the movie because it was too painful and too true. It was a larger-than-life version of her life, including all the screwed-up wrongs done by her husband, Dew—if that was his name, played by Tommy Lee Jones in dyed reddish-blond hair and eyebrows—all his drinking and carousing and philandering.

Another thing that got my attention in the movie—this was revealed in an interview that the director, Michael Apted, did with Loretta Lynn—was that Loretta wrote her songs while driving in the car to Nashville. That's the important truth that we don't learn anywhere in the movie but we do learn from what she tells us in the extras. She drove in her fancy Lincoln or Cadillac and she rhymed up her setbacks and her heartaches, and it all happened in her car.

I took the long way home, like Supertramp, and in the gloaming I saw a sign at a roadside farm stand. I used it in a song:

> Native peaches
> Fresh tomatoes
> Lots and lots of corn
>
> Hot blueberries
> Cold chicken
> And ridiculous amounts of porn

Then I stopped my Kia, my precious Korean Kia with one hundred and twenty-three thousand miles on it, on the road by a lumpy enormous green field. One spreading tree was left unfelled in the middle, as if in a painting by Constable. I could imagine the farmer resting his plow horse there in the shade on a hot day. Rounded shouldery boulders of last year's hay wrapped in white plastic were stacked off to one side. Every so often someone drove by in a red Subaru or a gray pickup with a lid over the back.

Tim said there isn't a good anti-drone song. I thought of trying to write it from the presidential point of view. I'd have President Obama sing something like "Today is Tuesday and I'm the warrior in chief. My people come into the office and we go down the list. I like to know who's going to die next. And I like the world to know that I'm a no-nonsense killer man who keeps us safe with robot planes. I like to go out afterward and have a smoke knowing I've decided which of my enemies I should kill. Sometimes little children are killed as well, and I'm sorry about that, but that's what happens, and I can't comment because it's classified security information. Today is Tuesday and I'm the warrior in chief."

But I know that would make for a terrible song—too on-the-nose. Too hard. Too angry. Too ungrieving. Griefs, not grievances, are what we need, said Robert Frost.

THERE'S AN INDUSTRIAL MACHINE made by the Sturtevant company called a Simpactor. I had a roommate long ago who had an internship at Sturtevant, and he talked about it in detail—interestingly, he was a big Talking Heads fan. He said there are several ways to grind things up fine: you can crush them between rollers or you can send them through an old-fashioned stone grinder, as in a flour mill, or—he lifted a finger—there's a machine called a Simpactor with a horizontal plate that spins. The coarse chunks fall onto the middle of the plate, where they are flung out toward a set of steel pins around the edge. Some of the pins are fixed and some are attached to the plate and move, and when the pins intersect they gnash and crush the crumbs of substance until it's just the right consistency. The Simpactor is useful for the pharmaceutical industry, my roommate said, because you need things ground very fine in order for them to be absorbed by the body. "That's fascinating," I said, "I had no idea." He didn't seem full of wonder at the Simpactor, though—he was much more interested in the Talking Heads concert that was coming up.

Tracy Chapman puts me through a moral Simpactor, breaking me into tiny pieces of uniform diameter so that I can absorb my own inadequacy. I think Tim may be wrong— "Change" may be the greatest protest song ever written. It's good partly because it offers no specific event or action. It's not protesting anything by name. It leaves it all up to you. It's just a series of questions. It asks these questions and prompts you to try to answer them, just as the Quakers ask questions. They have a list of questions called the Queries. Sometimes a woman reads one at Kittery Friends Meeting. One of the queries goes something like: Are you acting with love toward others? And I have to say, No, I'm not. Often I'm not. When I say catty things about Picasso or Ezra Pound, that psychotic, hateful fraud, I'm not bathed with generous feelings. When I imagine sneery songs about Barack Obama, I'm not a loving person at all.

I was making a second deviled-ham sandwich, using what remained in the can, and thinking about the importance of the inductive method, with "Change" on auto-repeat, when I heard some odd loud popping sounds. At first I thought they were something in the song that I hadn't noticed before, and then I realized that they were from outside the house. They seemed to be coming from the barn. I stopped the music and listened. I heard two loud explosions and then a sort of rolling thunder accompanied by an awful wooden twisting noise that didn't bode well at all. The dog was barking furiously. I went outside in time to see a large cloud of what looked like smoke ploofing out from the undercroft of the barn, down where I stored the canoe and my father's collection of plastic packaging.

I said some bad words. Was the barn on fire? Maybe caused by one of my Fausto cigars? No, it was a cloud of dust that was coming from underneath. I went up the ramp and pulled open the barn door, which takes almost superhuman strength because it sticks. Half of the first floor was gone, fallen down into the underbarn, and with it had tumbled about a hundred boxes of books and papers. Most of my collection of old anthologies was down there, the edges of the books visible from torn and squashed boxes—also my father's art books and his books on the history of chairs, and my mother's books of medieval history, and boxes of family photographs and letters—all mixed in with miscellaneous junk, a catcher's mitt, a sun-faded life jacket with mildew stains, my bicycle that I hadn't ridden yet this year because the chain is broken, Roz's old bicycle with the bent basket in front, scraps of plywood and planking, a sledgehammer. I saw one of my traveling sprinklers on its side, looking rusty and pathetic, on a box of something marked FRAGILE—STORE ON TOP. I was looking down at a huge hole in the barn with a lot of my life in it. I surveyed the scene for a moment and said, "Fuckaroo banzai." I didn't want to go below, in case more of the barn would give way and crush me dead.

I went inside and called Jeff, the barn repairman. A few years ago he'd fixed a sill that had been eaten to a punky powder by bugs. I left a message for him. "Hi, Jeff, it's Paul Chowder, I hope you're well. I've got a little situation here. Half the first floor of the barn has just collapsed. Things seem to be stable now, but I'd like you to take a look before I start hauling up the boxes." I left my cellphone number.

Then I went back out. I took another look at the damage and shook my head. I noticed, however, that the steps to the second floor were intact. By holding on to a wooden hook on the wall I was able to sidle sideways over to them and climb upstairs. My little music studio was fine. The microphone was pointing unperturbed at my empty white plastic chair. My keyboard was just where I'd left it. My guitar had slipped from where I'd leaned it against the table, but it was unharmed. I stood in the middle of the perfect second floor, with its neat pile of swept-together bird droppings under one of the tiny side-sliding windows that don't slide, and I laughed with relief. It's just boxes, I thought, it's just stuff. Everything's fine. Everything's just fine.

I WENT BACK to the house and gave Smack the rest of my sandwich and sat at the kitchen table for a while. Roz didn't answer her cellphone, so I left her a message. I called Allstate and told a nice woman with a Hispanic accent what had happened. She said, "I'm very sorry to hear about the damage to your barn. We can help you with that." She took down some details and told me to take pictures and said that a claims adjuster would be there later that afternoon. I thanked her and sat for a while longer. I took some pictures of the damage and wrote a paragraph for the record describing what had happened. I unrolled some wire fencing across the low entryway to the underbarn so that no pets or other animals would stray in. Then I climbed back up to the second floor. What the hell. Make some music in the wreckage.

Twenty

WHAT I REALLY WANT to do right now, I thought, is make a superfunkadelic dance beat. I want people to hear my music and smoke illicit substances and drink mojitos and chew Ecstasy, if that's what they do, and dance. I want to make people dance. I began layering a seventh-chord rhythm using the Steinway Hall, with another keyboard called Late Sixties Suitcase for the offbeats, and on the fourth offbeat I jabbed in a chord from a clavichord instrument called the Dry Funky Talker—a Stevie Wonder sort of instrument. On top I snuck in a flatted sixth chord for an extra magic-ass squirt of funkosity. I brought in a low, fast double hit for the bassline, a C and a D, using the Bottom Dweller Bass, and I reinforced it with steadily humpty-dumping quarter notes from a different instrument, the Progressive Rock Bass, at a hundred and twenty beats per minute. I was in the middle of quantizing the bassline—forcing it to stick exactly to the beat—when Roz called.

"Are you all right, baby?" she said.

I told her I was fine, that the barn was still standing, and that the insurance guy was coming.

"What about all the boxes? Your dad's books?"

"Not good. And the canoe is underneath them."

"Oh no, the canoe! What can I do? Can I come over?"

I knew she was very busy. "You're probably finishing a show."

"Well, it's kind of a madhouse here today. Nortin Hadler's scheduled for an interview. This is the first time he's been willing to talk to us. I could come later tonight."

"I'd love that," I said. "But it'll be late, and really I'm perfectly fine right now. You want to come this weekend? By then I'll know the damage."

She said she'd come on Saturday morning.

I said that would be great. I coughed.

"Are you still smoking cigars?" she asked.

"Yes, I am."

"Because that sounds like a dry cough. Is it a cigar cough?"

"No, I just swallowed some saliva." I coughed again.

"That's definitely a cigar cough," she said.

"Maybe it is. Mark Twain smoked twenty cigars a day. When he stopped, he wrote nothing. The man at the guitar store—I mean the cigar store—the man at the cigar store says that a cigar takes the serrated edge of life and makes it into a straight blade."

Roz said, "They'll be cutting a tumor out of your neck with a straight blade if you're not careful."

"Jesus, honey. Let's put that aside. It's just a temporary crutch. The music is the thing, and it's going forward at a hundred and twenty BPM. I'm hot, I'm smoking, I'm on a roll. In fact, I'm up on the second floor of the barn at this very minute writing a dance song."

"What? Come down from there. That's not safe. The floor just collapsed."

"You've got to take some risks in life."

"Please, baby, come down from the barn. Will you at least promise me you'll come down from the barn?"

"I promise. It's nice of you to worry."

She said good-bye. She's so thoughtful. It took three trips to move my equipment to the kitchen table. I clamped on my headphones and listened to what I had so far. It needed more. I went to work with the Trance Kit of sounds, which has a good kick drum and a nice synthesized clap with a hint of rimshot in it for the second and fourth beats. Then I had an idea: I played the plink of the egg slicer on top with some echo synced to the eighth notes. Tasty. I brought another chord rhythm on the Funky Talker. It sounded pretty good, frankly. I laughed and pursed my lips and windmilled my arms. It was pure retro Stevie Wonder, but with a dance beat.

Now I needed some vocals. I hooked up the pre-amp and adjusted the microphone so that it was right at my mouth, and I sang random things. "Egg slicer, ooh, ooh! Slice that egg, ooh, ooh!" Then: "Guan—tan—a—moe-hoh!" I ran my voice through Logic's phone filter so that it sounded not like me. I sang, "Why can't you close—Guantanamo?" Then: "Make no mistake—you betrayed our faith." I'm so tired of hearing Obama say "Make no mistake." "Make no mistake," he said in his Nobel Peace Prize speech, "evil does exist in the world." Which is why he has to ship arms to Libyan rebels and fly drones around everywhere and spread violence and kill people. It's sickening. Make no mistake? His whole foreign policy is one long string of mistakes. And we're supposed to get excited about health care. More tests, more drugs, more colonoscopies, more needless invasive procedures. Fuck it!

Then I thought of a stanza in a Charles Causley poem. I hit the space bar to begin my egg slicer loop and I sang

> O war is a casual mistress
> And the world is her double bed.
> She has a few charms in her mechanised arms
> But you wake up and find yourself dead.

That was much better than any lyric I could write. Causley's father died of injuries suffered in World War I. Could I make a hot bumping antiwar dance song out of Causley's stanza? Probably not, but even if I could, they wouldn't be my words. I'd have to get permission from his executor, and it would be a whole wrangle. I had to supply my own lyrics.

I WAS OUT by the half-dead apple tree dancing to Phatso Brown's remix of "Apes from Space" when the man from Allstate arrived with his clipboard. I showed him the scene of the accident. He made some measurements and took a lot of photographs. He was an enthusiast of post-and-beam construction with a beard, and he seemed to know what he was looking at. He asked about the heap of boxes. "They're mostly just old papers and books and probably they're fine," I said. "As long as it doesn't rain." The underbarn has a sand floor and it floods when there's a heavy rain. There was a canoe down there, too, I added—only a bit of it was visible. He asked about its value.

"What can I say?" I said. "Green fiberglass canoe, Old Town, some happy hours on the river. It probably cost a thousand dollars. Maybe more. It was a birthday present from my ex-girlfriend." He nodded and made a note. I left him to perform further calculations and sat in the white plastic chair making an intensive auditory study of the dance songs in my iTunes library. There are so many great dance songs—and yet there's room for more. Or so I thought. I wanted to start a dance song with a woman saying, "And I'll see *you* later." Maybe I could convince Roz to say it. I listened to "Safe from Harm" by Andrew Bennett, and "Save the Last Trance for Me" by Paul Oakenfold, and "Healing of the Nation" by Sherman, and "La Luna" by Blank & Jones, and "Striptease in Istanbul" by Nublu Sound, and parts of four songs by Underworld.

Underworld is good. I discovered them by chance on a long plane flight. I was poking at the touch screen, looking for something to listen to after watching a very good documentary on Picasso and Matisse—Matisse comes off well, and after his operation he uses a pair of large shears to cut colored pieces of paper—and I saw a song on a list called "Bigmouth." It was a dance number with an insanely honking harmonica and no words, and it was by Underworld, a band who had also created something called "Mmm . . . Skyscraper I Love You." Back in the eighties they were doing things I would like to have done—chopping up found voice clips ahead of the game—although they were too tolerant perhaps in their early days of zappy saw-toothed sounds, as everyone was. The song I liked best by them was a more recent one called "Bird 1." "Bird 1" is about something—I don't know what— something about a white stick and a shaft of sunlight and a fly and a chainsaw of tiny firecrackers. I'm always a sucker for a shaft of sunlight. It's stoned, I guess. It's "poetry." The chorus is splendid. "There is one bird in my house," sings the main Underworld man, Karl Hyde. Not "a bird," but "one bird." There's basically only one chord for most of the song, as well as one bird. There are a great many words in the song, however. Most of them don't rhyme, and as in many great songs, the words aren't terribly important. I would like to write something like this.

Where is my lighter? I'm simply unable to light a cigar

stub outdoors with just a match. I haven't mastered the technique.

The Allstate man said he had everything he needed. He said it looked like about five thousand dollars' worth of structural damage, plus eighteen hundred for the books and the canoe—assuming the canoe was a total loss—and he'd be able to get me a check this week. We shook hands and he drove away. He had a sticker on his window that read "Proud Parent of an Honor Student." I liked him.

IT'S EVENING NOW. Some fine fleshy clouds. I've squandered an hour setting Lewis Carroll's "Soup of the Evening" to music. My mother used to read that poem to me and laugh and say how good it was, and it is awfully good. My tune may be marginally better than the one that Willy Wonka sings in one of the movie versions of *Alice in Wonderland*, and then again it may not. And the question is, Do we need another musical version of "Soup of the Evening"? I'm soaked with sweat.

All songs are protest songs, as somebody once observed— was it Bob Dylan? Every song presupposes enough peace and quiet that the song itself can be sung, the guitar strummed, the words heard. There's no way people can be dancing if there are explosions and cries of anguish outside. In fact, most people are peaceable most of the time, regardless of what they say. Yeats says, "Our master Caesar's in the tent, the maps are all outspread. His eyes are fixed upon nothing, his hands under his head." Something like that. In other words, Caesar is lying very still. He may be planning mayhem and flank attacks and organized massacre, but he needs quiet while he strategizes. The poem is called "Long-Legged Fly." If you're a stop-lossed land warrior getting drunk in your Humvee listening to "Beer for My Horses" to get hepped up for a retributive foray into some tiny dirt-poor village in Afghanistan, you're just a person sitting in a Humvee while that song is playing. Even if you're the biggest, meanest, tattooedest thug of a bar-brawling jackalope who beats up defenseless people every other night, even if you hate music and never listen to it, you need to eat and sleep and recover from the cuts and bruises on your knuckles and regain your pointless rage. You are nonviolent except for the brief periods when you're violent. For what that's worth. I called Tim and tried this line of reasoning out on him and he wasn't terribly impressed. He's gone hyperpolitical because it's an election year.

He said, "Why don't you write a book about trying to write a protest song?"

"I guess I sort of am," I said.

I'm having problems writing lyrics. They're either too simple, or too clever-clever, or too sexual. It's reassuring to go back to listening to dance songs, because usually there are very few words. In one of Paul Oakenfold's songs there are five words at the beginning, shouted by a television preacher: "I said praise the Lord!" After a while there's a recorded outgoing message from a woman from 976-4PRAYER. That's it. And it's a good song. A good protest song.

Twenty-one

I DON'T WANT TO GO TO BED YET. My piano technique is getting a little better, I think. I learned to play piano on our beat-up, difficult-to-tune Chickering, with carved floral decoration. Some of the keys had cigarette burns or missing ivories or both. I took lessons with Mrs. Trebert, who explained to me that her name was unusual because it was the same backward and forward. Bach would have liked her name: it was a backward canon at the unison. It was her husband's name, actually. He was very sick and pale and quiet. He sat in a warm, dark room while Mrs. Trebert listened to me play Bach and Béla Bartók. My favorite piece was by Bartók, in A minor. The left hand went back and forth between two notes, an A and an E, and the right hand played something equally uncomplicated. Béla Bartók was a Hungarian composer who was hired by Koussevitzky to write a piece for orchestra that has a gigantic solo for three bassoons. When Bartók was in Europe he wrote dissonant, despairing pieces, but for Koussevitzky he wrote something sunny and accessible and immortal.

One week, when I went to have a lesson, Mrs. Trebert said her husband had passed away. She cried and I felt that I was shrinking to the size of a cashew in the presence of such unfathomable unhappiness.

My failure to practice also made her sad, and only six months after her husband died I told my parents that I didn't want to have piano lessons anymore. Instead I learned to play the bassoon. I learned a lot of terminology, like "senza vibrato," which I thought meant "with vibrato" but actually means "without vibrato." Vibrato is just when you add a wobble to a note. You can wobble the note by making it louder or softer, say with your diaphragm if you're a singer or a wind player, or by moving the pitch up and down slightly with the rockings of your abused fingertips if you're a string player or Segovia. Electric guitar players get to use a special twanger to stretch the strings and produce vibrato, which is how Jimi Hendrix played "The Star-Spangled Banner." Opera singers sometimes use too much vibrato and it drives everyone mad.

What is a note? A note is a sound represented by a black blob on the page. Notes can be long or short, and in real life they are always bending up and down like flexible claymation figures. I had a bad dream once in which I was a successful composer of scores for horror movies. I'd written a very frightening and suspenseful track for a chase scene where a man tries to protect a woman from a disfigured eyeless monster—or so I reconstruct the setting—but the movie that I'd scored so well was never released and the chase scene music had nowhere to go, and was condemned to wander the world pursuing people. In the dream I woke up, and in the dimness of the room I saw the chase scene music there hovering at the foot of my bed—a shadowy humanoid made of writhingly alive notes like long black water balloons. It had found me. I got up and tried to touch the notes and that made them angry. The chase scene music began chasing me, with terrible violin-harmonic screeching sounds and glissandi from the double basses. The music could find no peace. It was an awful dream. Fortunately I don't have nightmares that often.

So a note can be long or short. When Paul McCartney sings, "Blackbird singing in the dead of night," the "of" is a slide upward. It could be written as two notes on the page, but it's sung as a single upward-swooping sound. When Marvin Gaye sings "bay-eee-eee-bee-eee" in "Sexual Healing," there are five distinctly audible notes, and yet nobody is counting them because numbers have nothing to do with sexual healing. Each of the "notes" has been healed by being annealed, that is, by being melted into the next note, and you can hear that Marvin Gaye knew that this song, cowritten with an admiring journalist, was going to be an enormous hit, bigger than anything else he'd done, even though his life was sliding downhill.

Sung notes are always sliding uphill and downhill into

each other because it's not possible for a human voice to leap from one note to the next instantaneously. But why are they called notes? I don't know. I guess a note is a little memorandum to self, a way of remembering a melody. A melody is a tune—something you can hum—like a move in chess. You can hum a tune but you can't hum the harmony underneath a tune, and you can't hum a clever sacrifice in a chess game, even though you can write Bxd6. If you look at old musical scores, from the fifteenth century, they write the notes as little diamond shapes on a stave. Meanwhile the itinerant jongleurs were singing and clapping and writing nothing down. Having assignations in the beer pantry.

What's a stave? Ah, the stave is the set of five lines onto which you hang the notes. There's the E line, the G line, the B line, the D line, and the F train. I was taught a helpful mnemonic: Every Good Boy Does Fine. It's not true, though. Some good boys do not do that well in school. Or in life. There's also Elvis's Guitar Broke Down Friday, and Earth Girls Blow Dairy Farmers—no, I made that last one up. You're putting the notes out for display on the staves. You are in fact espaliering the notes like a pear tree on a wooden frame. If you put the note up here on Friday, it's going to be higher in "pitch," meaning higher up on the pitch of the slope. And if you pin the note on Elvis down here, it's going to be lower in pitch, because up is vocal constriction and tension and upwardness and mountaintops, and lower is moon river and the bass singer in the Four Tops.

So the stave, or staff, is simply five lines of wooden framing onto which you hang the notes for the sake of convenience. And the really confusing thing is that middle C is not located in the middle of the stave, it's below the stave. Middle C is a key next to two black keys roughly in the middle of the piano keyboard. It's the center of everything and yet perversely it's represented as a note below the first line of the staff, or stave—a note with a little line through it to signal that there's a virtual line below the five lines, so that it looks like a flying saucer.

And then there are bar lines—vertical lines that neatly cross the stave every so often. They form measures, which are little aquariums of time in which the notes must forever swim. At first there were no bar lines, because the choristers figured that all you needed to know was the tune. If you're singing a monkish chant you just need to be reminded of the tune. But then they began working out a code for longer notes and shorter notes—shorter notes were black blobs and longer notes were open blobs that weren't colored in—and then they resorted to fiddling with the tail of the notes, so that some notes were so-called quarter notes, which were very important because they fell on every beat, and they had upsticking or downsticking single tails, while eighth notes had curvy spinnakers off their poles and if they joined up with other eighth notes they were united by angled bars between their poles as if they were going by too fast to stand on their own, and sixteenth notes had a second droopy thing, or a second connecting bar. The angled bars that connect notes are different from the vertical bar lines that separate measures—very confusing. I'm falling apart here.

Another oddity of nomenclature: A piano key is a physical object that is different from the key, or "key signature," that the music is in. A piece of music may be in the key of C major but the melody might begin on the D key or the E key or any key at all. Debussy called the piano a "box of hammers." "The Sunken Cathedral" is in the key of C major, more or less.

But the main thing to keep in mind is that the melody, or tune, the hummable essence of a song, is like a thread that is wrapped around various doorknobs in a large ornate eighteenth-century room of harmony designed by an architect named Rameau, and the knobs of harmony are made up of groups of constitutive notes called chords, and each chord has a little positive or negative ionic charge in it that moves things forward with colorn;;;;;"" 'n

I seem to have fallen asleep.

JEFF THE BARN MAN and two of his guys showed up first thing in the morning, and we set up a ladder and a bucket brigade and started rescuing the boxes and putting them in a back part of the first floor of the barn where the crossbeams had several upright supports. By the fiftieth book box Jeff said, "I think I'm getting a better sense of why the floor collapsed." A carton of my family letters had broken open— postcards from uncles and aunts, and birthday wishes, and a

"Dear Grandmother and Grandfather" thank-you from me, in blue felt-tip pen, for the Mediterranean cruise. "The Parthenon was ineffable," I'd written. I remembered my mother suggesting the word to me when, sitting at the kitchen table, I'd asked her for something that meant "mysterious."

One of my three traveling sprinklers had its sprayer arms mangled, but my father's original Sears model was in fine shape. And, miraculously, his collection of plastic packaging, egg cartons and foam clamshell boxes and appliance-cradling abstract shapes of Styrofoam, was completely untouched— stretch-wrapped in clear plastic sheeting on a pallet out of range of the avalanche. The canoe, however, was totally squashed. "Yep, I'd say you're not going to get very far in that," said Jeff. I dragged it out onto the grass and swore and took a picture of it to email to the Allstate man.

One lucky thing: I found my silver and blue paperback copy of Howard Moss's *Selected Poems*, which I'd been looking for for years. It had somehow found its way into a U-Haul box with some very old, very fat *New Yorker*s. The box burst, and there was the Howard Moss paperback. On the back of the book was a blurb from James Merrill: "Over the years Howard Moss has arrived, with next to no luggage, at mastery." Inside was an ancient, faded dot-matrix-printed receipt on stiff paper from a cash machine operated by the Bank of New England: on June 7, 1980, I withdrew sixty dollars. Where are those dollars now? Gone to graveyards every one.

Jeff said he would write up an estimate for the floor repair, but he said that five thousand from Allstate would certainly cover it. The three of them drove off, their pickup trucks filled with broken planking. I took Smack for a walk and gave him a liver snack, which made his morning, and then I went out for breakfast at the Friendly Toast. The box lifting had made me hungry and I ordered the Irish eggs Benedict, made with corned beef hash instead of a circular disk of ham. Then, for the first time in more than thirty years, I read Howard Moss's poem "Piano Practice." I'd forgotten how observant it was. "The left hand's library is dull," Moss says, "the books / All read, though sometimes, going under velvet, / An old upholsterer will spit out tacks." That's very true about the low register of the piano. Partway through, Moss has an underwater stanza about Debussy, which unfortunately ends on a less good note about how the deep-sea mirrors "eat their hearts out." Scratch that—I even like Moss's mirror image now. It's all done in a loose-seeming pentameter, with a great deal more enjambment than is healthy, but never mind the meter: you can practically hear the ice cubes in Moss's scotch glass tinkle as he's writing—writing and listening through layers of lath and plaster to his neighbor the industrious student musician.

I remember how glum I was after reading "Piano Practice" for the first time all those years ago. I'd been working on and off for a year on a poem about piano playing, trying to describe the mingled sounds I heard coming from the practice rooms while I waited for my reed to soak, and Howard Moss's poem made mine superfluous. Now, though, his poem only made me happy.

Twenty-two

RAYMOND'S GOT GENUINE MUSICAL TALENT—I've got his "beans in my jeans" song running through my head.

I'm sitting on a wet beach towel in the car with raindrops popping away on the roof. The driver's seat was soaked because last night I forgot to roll up the window all the way. That's what a Fausto cigar will do to you. You crack the window to let some smoke out, then it rains all night long, and boom, your ass is wet. I think I should stop inhaling. I've got another beach towel draped down from the roof of the car so that more rain won't come in the window. It's the only thing I don't like about this car—no gutters. Thank goodness the barn boxes are all up and safe.

The textbook I'm currently reading is by Rick Snoman, a DJ and remixer, and it's called *Dance Music Manual*. It's got 522 pages and it's arranged like a scholastic treatise on angels and is about as helpful to an amateur musician like me as Aquinas's *Summa Theologica* would be. Here's what I've learned so far. There are eight genres of dance music: House, Trance, UK Garage, Techno, Hip-hop, Trip-hop, Ambient, and Drum 'n Bass. Trip-hop? House music arose in the eighties as disco was dying, Snoman writes: "DJ Nicky Siano set up a New York club known as The Gallery, and hired Frankie Knuckles and Larry Levan to prepare the club for the night by spiking the drinks with lysergic acid diethylamide." Trance, on the other hand, started in the nineties with a song by DJ Dag and Jam El Mar called "We Came in Peace," which repeats a single phrase from the Apollo 11 moon message several dozen times. It was intended to create a state of trance but it doesn't seem to work—there's such a thing as too much Neil Armstrong. The genre quickly evolved, according to Snoman: "The increased popularity of 3,4-methylenedioxy-N-methylamphetamine (MDMA or 'E') amongst clubbers inevitably resulted in new forms of trance being developed." Ambient music could be traced back, he says, to a moment in the mid-seventies "when Brian Eno was run over by a taxi." In the hospital Eno listened to some harp music while rain beat gently on the windowpane, and he liked the intermixture, and there you go. In the index to Snoman's book, Daft Punk appears as "Punk, Daft." Prince doesn't appear in the index at all.

Here's my one-week dance-music self-study boot-camp syllabus. From the seventies, we begin with a formal analysis of Donna Summer singing "I Feel Love." Moving her bad-girl hips and looking up at the lord in that wicked, innocent way she has. Boom, done. We move on to the total sonar-echo funkosity of the Talking Heads doing "Take Me to the River." Boom. We decide to turn up the volume slightly, because everything sounds better louder. From the eighties, we rediscover Chaka Khan doing "Ain't Nobody," with carbon-neutral keyboard sequences by Hawk Wolinski, and "Talking in Your Sleep" by the Romantics, boom, living in a spotlight, boom. Then the Fixx, very tight, doing "Saved by Zero." Then Midnight Star, "No Parking on the Dance Floor" and "Operator," boom, boom, "Operator, this is an emergency." We begin to feel a powerful sense of obligation: we *must dance*. Then we study the inscrutable a cappella chord that begins "She's Strange" by Cameo, and we try unsuccessfully to make harmonic sense of the meanderingly slow arousing siren wail that follows. Next we turn our attention to the Crystal Method doing "Vapor Trail," which seems to be about smoking crack although there are no words and it's just as good sober, boom diddly boom. We turn up the volume further and spend an hour worshipping the chorus of Underworld's "Always Loved a Film," and then we bring the noise with Benny Benassi's remix of Public Enemy, boom. We sit cross-legged, devoting an afternoon to the greatness of Hol Baumann doing "Bénarès" and Mercan Dede doing "Ab-i Hayat"—boom, boom, dakka doom, doom sa, comme ça—and then we pound our delighted hippocampuses with Eric Prydz's ode to the piano, "Pjanoo." At the final reception cast party we all dance to George

Clinton's "Atomic Dog" until we must chase the cat. Then we collapse in orgiastic confusion, knowing that we have a good solid foundation for getting down on it. Tuition: the cost of fifteen songs on iTunes.

ROZ JUST LEFT. I'm in shock. I said, "Before we look at the barn and get all sad, I want to try out a song on you." I played her my Guantanamo song, which I'd fiddled with a bit. She dipped her knees to it here and there, which pleased me. After it was over, she said, "It's got a great dance beat, but I'm honestly just not sure about the Guantanamo part, because it's so upbeat and cheerful that it seems as if you're almost making fun of Guantanamo, which is surely not what you mean. Guantanamo is a terrible prison where people are forced to waste their lives. Shouldn't the song be something more like—I don't know, 'I saw you on the dance floor, / I never wanted anything more, / I bought a rubber at the corner store'?"

"That's it!" I said, writing her lyrics on a folded-up piece of paper. I also played her a fresh version of the doctor song. She liked that one.

Then I showed her the missing barn floor and the squashed-flat canoe, which was still out on the grass. She surprised me by starting to cry.

"It moved so smoothly over the water," she said.

"I'm sorry, honey," I said, holding her. "I'm sorry the barn failed. I'm sorry about the canoe. I'm sorry things turned out this way. Come inside, let's not look at this anymore. I've got a bottle of blackstrap molasses for you."

She looked up at me. Then she gave me the shock. It wasn't what I expected. It wasn't about Harris the doctor.

"I HAVE SOMETHING TO TELL YOU," she said. "It technically doesn't affect you, but it does."

"What?" I steeled myself. If she was going to say she was engaged, I simply wasn't going to accept it.

She said, "I think I'm going to have a hysterectomy."

My mouth opened and closed. "You mean they're going to—" I didn't finish.

"Remove it," she said. "Not my ovaries, just the, ah, uterus. Just the center of it all."

I stared at her, horrified.

"I told you it's not cancer, it's really not," Roz said. "Sweetie, don't look at me that way. It's not malignant, and I'm not going to die. I have uterine growths called fibroids. Lots of women have them and they're usually not a problem. But I've got, it turns out, a whole bunch of them, in a knot— like a baobob tree. You know that big tree in *Avatar*? That's what it feels like I've got in me."

"How absolutely awful." I clutched her arm. "And there's no other way?"

"We've tried several things, they were a waste of time. The gynecologist has been telling me I should have the hysterectomy right away, but I've resisted it. She says I'll feel ten times better if we go ahead—the bloodletting will stop, the pain will stop, the anemia will go away. The fibroid is giving me the horrible periods, because it's so big and gnarly. It means well, but it's killing me."

"You poor dear thing."

"My last hope was that I'd hit menopause and it would disappear on its own. But no luck. It loves estrogen. It just keeps on growing. And it aches."

"Oh, baby," I said. I put my arms around her. "Have you told Harris?"

"Harris is a minimalist and he's been telling me I should wait and exhaust every alternative—he's been a bit rigid on the subject, actually. But now even he's saying I should do it. I probably should have had it done a year ago."

"Come on inside," I said. "Let me make some tea."

We walked into the house. "I know I'm really too old to have a baby," she said, "but to lose your own womb—the place where little babies grow—" She held back her grief. "It's just so final. Sorry."

"Sh, sh, it's okay, it's okay," I said. As I stroked her arm I was seized by a paroxysm of remorse. This was my fault. I put some water on the stove, thinking furiously. "Can I feel it?" I said.

"No, Paul. Please. It's private."

"I know, forget it, I'm sorry. It's just that we should have had a kid. We'd be together now if we'd had a kid, and you wouldn't have this horrible feeling of finality. I'm so sorry."

Roz said, "I'd probably still be facing this whether or not

we'd had a child. You didn't want to have a child when I wanted to and so we didn't. That's just what happened."

I put a tea bag in a mug. "What can I do for you?"

"Well, probably nothing. I just have to face up to it, and I thought you should know." She smiled at me through tears. "You could hold me."

I held her and stroked her back. I felt the wrinkles in her shirt and the slight thickness of her bra clasp.

"And I'll take that bottle of molasses," she said.

Twenty-three

O<small>H, ME.</small> That good, good woman. I spent all morning reading the message boards in hysterectomy support groups. A lot of women said that having a hysterectomy was the best decision they'd ever made. Others were unhappy because they'd wanted to have a second child, or a third child. Or just a child.

Once on a hot night when Roz and I were watching a documentary called *Dark Days*, I got the big square fan and plugged it in and said we could cool our loins with it. Then I asked her whether women had loins, as men did. Was it a gender-neutral term? She said, "I think so, technically. It's anything in the upper thigh area and anything that is carried or tucked away between the thighs." Then she said, "When I was little I always misread 'loin cloth' as 'lion cloth.' I thought Hercules killed the lion and then wore the fur over his privates. The dyslexic mistake is part of the meaning."

"He girded his lion," I said. I turned on the fan. The documentary was about people living in shacks in an underground rail tunnel in New York City. It was a very good movie, but it made Roz sad. Here is a world with so much disparity and so much striving and suffering, she thought, and what am I doing with my life? I think that movie was part of what got her to apply for the producer job at the radio show.

I WORKED for several hours today on a new song called "Honk for Assistance." I saw the sign at a convenience store, near the ice machine, and I thought, Now, *that* is a dance song, in the tradition of Midnight Star. I sampled a few honks from my Kia's horn and set up a beat and fingered up some harmony using an instrument I hadn't tried before, the Gospel Organ, which has a slight percussive sound in the attack phase of each note. I added more chords on a Mark II keyboard and some homegrown handclaps and some rhythms made with the Funk Boogie Kit. And then I wondered idly whether somebody had already made a song out of "Honk for Assistance." Yes, they had. The composer's name was Tom Clark and it was on an EP called *Nervous*. It's pretty good. No words. Foolish me: You must never look anything up on iTunes while you're working on a song. Otherwise you'll stop and you'll say it's all been done.

I need money. Money always helps. I called Gene and told him that my book of poems, formerly called *Misery Hat*, was turning out to be something different. It was now a book about music.

"Ah, okay."

"It seems to be about trying to write dance songs. Also protest songs and love songs. Pop songs in general."

"Maybe we could do an enhanced ebook and include the songs."

That depended, I said, on whether the songs were any good or not.

"Whether they're good doesn't matter," Gene said. "Process not product, as they say about schoolchildren. Just give it the Chowder spin. And stay away from the misery hat."

When that check comes from Allstate I'm going to buy Roz a new canoe. That's the least I can do.

WHEN DEBUSSY WAS YOUNG he wanted to write music for women to sing. He wrote love songs and he wrote erotic songs. He set some of Pierre Louÿs's *Chansons de Bilitis* to music, Louÿs who late in life wrote a poem called "The Trophy of Legendary Vulvas"—what a title! When I was young and wanted to be a composer like Debussy, I paid no attention to any of his songs. I couldn't listen to them. I listened only to his piano and orchestral music. The only vocals of his that I could stand were the wordless vowels that the sirens sing in the *Nocturnes*, and even those I wasn't sure about. I still can't listen to his songs with any pleasure. The words seem pushed and pulled and crowded by the music. But that's my loss.

Everything for Debussy was really about sex and smoking. Sex, smoking, the grand piano, and the English Channel. Those were his mainstays. He fell in love with his singers all through his life. One of his earliest songs repeats the line "The sea is deep" several times—it's dedicated to Madame Vasnier, a singer. He may or may not have had an affair with Mary Garden, the woman who sang in his opera *Pelléas and Mélisande*. In her memoir, Mary Garden says nothing happened between them, but she's not convincing. Debussy liked Scottish women with gentle voices who hung around wells, and he liked women who had flaxen hair—he wrote a lovely piano prelude called "The Girl with the Flaxen Hair," which was inspired by his first wife, Lilly, who wounded herself with a handgun after Debussy took up with the brown-haired woman who became his second wife. He liked brown-haired women, too. He just plain liked women. Women and moonlight and *vers libre* and smoking strong French cigarettes. And then he died broke and miserable. His new wife's father had disinherited her.

You never want to have cancer down there, where Debussy had it. Cancer of the rectum. Cancer of the anus. I guess we would now call it colon cancer.

But thank heaven Debussy was poor, because the poverty forced him to finish twelve preludes in 1910. I remember the first time I heard the sixth prelude, "Footsteps in the Snow." I immediately wanted to understand how he did it, and I couldn't. He was using a different scale, the so-called whole-tone scale—that was part of it. Instead of a normal scale, which has a few half tones thrown in here and there, he used a scale composed entirely of whole tones. But anyone can do that. He made it sound cold and bleak, with wind-eroded oval footprints. I remember dropping the needle down and hearing, along with the scratched vinyl, the empty world of whiteness and snow and almost effaced footprints that he created.

Maurice Ravel knew immediately how good Debussy's *Preludes* were. Ravel was an inspired pianist, and he played them for himself in May 1910, just when they were published. He was struggling at the time with the orchestration of a piece of his own that was going slowly, and he hadn't always gotten along with Debussy, but he put all that aside. "I will console myself by playing Debussy's *Preludes* once again," he wrote to a friend. "They are wonderful masterpieces. Do you know them? Thank you, and cordially in haste, Maurice Ravel."

Twenty-four

HELLO, HELLO. I'm sitting by the side of the Piscataqua River admiring the power station across the way, with its beautiful white plumes of steam or smoke that warm the earth. The beach that I'm sitting at is called Dead Duck Beach. It's misty again today, with a determined but thwarted sun leaving a splotch of brightness on the water, which is salty, because the Piscataqua is a tidal river. About a hundred yards from me a little boy wearing a bright red vest is throwing handfuls of sand into the water and calling out things I can't hear.

I had one of the worst nights of my life last night. I went to dinner at my sister's house and was amazed all over again by her two tall grown children. I looked at them and thought, I should have been a better uncle to these two extraordinary children. My sister never asks me about the money that I owe her. I owe her money from when I was working on the anthology. I've got to pay her back.

Fortunately she's got a new husband who has lots of money because he was a patent lawyer in Washington for many years. He said he stopped patent lawyering because the system had become hopelessly corrupt—the patent office was interested in making billions in fees by issuing as many patents as possible, and the lawyers wanted ambiguities and mistakes in the patents granted so that they could bring infringement suits against one another. Also his eyes were bad and he didn't want to stare at the computer screen all day looking at scanned versions of old patents.

I was sad to learn that the patent office was corrupt, and I ate too much of the eggplant tapenade I brought as a present and was poisoned by the garlic, and when I got home to bed five thousand unrelated thoughts traipsed through my brain and I worried about Roz and grieved over not having a child and got almost no sleep. Finally I went down to the kitchen and smoked a Fausto and made a dance loop and a serviceable chorus that went, in a ZZ Top sort of accent, "Take a ride in my boat." I went to bed at five a.m. and I woke up and coughed a lot. I decided that I would go to the convenience store to get some cough drops. Honk for assistance. While I was unwrapping a cough drop I remembered something Roz always used to say before she went out for a shop at the supermarket. She'd say, in a hopeful, cheery, loving voice, "Anything you need at the store that I don't know about?" The memory of her voice skewered clean through me and I thought, This is ridiculous. I know Roz. I know that woman. I know everything about her. She knows everything about me. We've lived together. We've been canoeing together. We've watched large basking toads jump off a sunlit branch on the river as we floated by. This doctor she's dating now hardly knows her. He hasn't been canoeing with her. He's no good for her. It's as simple as that. Tony Hoagland indeed.

I've filmed some boats with my video camera, thinking that I could make a YouTube video of "Take a Ride in My Boat" if I had some verses. I used some of the three-syllable phrases Roz had sent me, adjusting them here and there:

> hear the word
> get up soon
> kiss the lips
> bite the moon
>
> feel the fruit
> find your way
> sail the boat
> dream of me
>
> Take a ride in my boat
> Take a ride
> Take a ride in my boat
>
> fix the text
> take the stick

crack the nut
make it slick

chomp the bit
drink the beer
wipe the spit
check the gear

crack the nut and drop the pants
milk the meat and learn to dance

Take a ride in my boat
Take a ride
Take a ride in my boat
Take a ride in my boat
Take a ride in my boat
Take a ride in my boat

I TOOK THE CAR in to a repair place to be inspected. They looked at it for an hour and the man said it needed new calipers and pads and several other expensive things. The total cost would be about twenty-five hundred dollars. "For that car, I don't think it's worth it," he said.

"I see, okay," I said.

"Just call me Dr. Carvorkian," he said.

I took it to another repair place farther away. When I got there the head of service was in the glass-walled waiting room sitting next to an elderly woman. I waited for about five minutes at the service counter, and I saw the man nodding sympathetically, listening to a long story that the woman was telling him. Finally he came out and said, "Sorry, I was talking to that lady." I told him my problem with the brakes. He was a young-faced, perky, smiley man, and he said they'd take a look.

I went into the waiting room. The old woman was still there waiting. "It's nice and cool in here," I said.

"Yes, it is, almost too cool," she said. She asked me what kind of car I had, and I told her. "We've always had American cars," she said. "But my husband passed away in 2006 and last year a woman backed into the trunk of my old Lincoln. The damage wasn't too bad, but when I got home the car caught fire in the garage and it was totaled. I bought a new Lincoln but I don't like it as much."

Then she went away and I waited an hour. The perky man came in and said, "Looks good, there was almost nothing. Your brake fluid was a little low and the brake lines are rusty, so we're going to need to keep an eye on that. But the calipers are almost new, so that's good." He passed me a sheet of paper. The total for labor was $77.90 and the total for parts was $14.35. So my car has passed inspection and it's good for another year. Another year of life in my car! You just need to find the right serviceman.

I INVITED Nan and Raymond over for a second round of sushi, hoping that Raymond might teach me some tricks with pitch bending, but Nan said no. Raymond was in Boston seeing his girlfriend at Emerson College. I asked Nan how life was treating her.

"Oh, my mother died," she said softly.

I said how sorry I was.

"I'm going to miss her. She was a real fighter. She just had too many different things going wrong at the same time. My sister was there. She said it was peaceful." Nan was going back to Toronto briefly, she said, to help sort things out and sign forms, but the memorial service wouldn't be for several weeks. "Fortunately Chuck has lots of frequent flyer miles."

"You were a good daughter to her."

I heard her sigh. After a while, she said, "I hope so. I guess I'll be needing some help with the chickens, if you could."

"Absolutely, glad to do it. The rooster seems to like me. And I'm serious about watering the tomatoes."

"That would be nice, thank you. And ask Raymond about his songs, if you get a chance."

Twenty-five

HELLO AND WELCOME to Chowder's Poetry Hopalong.
I'm your host and in-home chiropodist, Paul Chowder.
We're in my kitchen, and I'm talking into a seven-hundred-
dollar microphone. My ex-girlfriend is probably going to
have a major operation, and my neighbor's mother has died.
So that's what's happening, and it's serious business.

Out of worry or trouble or despair must come some
enlightenment. Maybe that's what a chord progression can
teach us. Out of the shuffling mess of dissonance comes a
return to pax, to the three-note triad of something basic and
pure and unable to be argued with. Chong: the chord. E flat
major. A flat major. C sharp minor. Chords where only the
middle finger is down on the flat ground of the white keys,
while up on top the pinky maybe can't resist adding an impish
hint of misdirection—an added seventh or ninth. These are
just fancy terms for willful blurring—they're like the times

when the attractive magician's helper in the leotard disappears into the box and the magician plunges all his sharp swords in, and then she reappears with outstretched arms, smiling her E flat major smile, unscathed after her chordal perils. Debussy's preludes go all over the place, but they're tonal—they always come back home.

Music notation relies on things called sharps and things called flats. A sharp looks sharp and spiky—it's the pound sign on the typewriter, the one above the number 3. A flat looks melted, like a droopy wasp's abdomen with a line sticking up from it. The round side of the flat symbol points to the right on the stave, whereas the water-balloon notes all point to the left, looking back at where they've been. If you see a sharp printed in front of a note, you know to look sharp and shift that note's pitch up by a half step, whereas if you see a flat in front of a note, you know to droop down flat a half step. So if you see a good-boy G on the stave with a wasp in front of it, that's a G flat. That's chess notation. It works, and we can thank the monks and the madrigalists for it. But when you're making up a melody, you don't think about sharps and flats. You wave them away. You don't even necessarily think about chord progressions.

There's a famous chord progression that goes, in Roman numerals, I, V, vi, IV, I. Meaning that if you're in C major it begins with a major chord based on the first note of the scale, C, then goes to a major chord built on the fifth note of the scale, G, then to a minor chord on the sixth note, A, then to a major chord on the fourth note, F, then back to a C chord.

Schumann used this chord progression, Brahms used it, Elton John used it, the Beatles used it in "Let It Be," Jason Mraz used it in "I'm Yours," and Alphaville and Mr. Hudson and Jay-Z used it in "Forever Young," and on and on. A group called the Axis of Awesome made a medley of many songs based on these chords—fifty million people have watched versions of the Axis of Awesome medley on YouTube. It's worth watching.

You may think you have something extremely useful when you know how to play these four chords, and you do. But when you're at the point of making up a tune that's never been heard before, and finding words for it to shoulder, then knowing the chords doesn't help that much. You still have to feel your way singingly through.

ROZ'S CELLPHONE WENT right to voicemail, so I called her home number. Her doctor friend Harris answered. I recognized his voice from the radio. I said, "Hello, this is Paul Chowder. Is that—Harris?"

"Yes," said Harris.

"Hi, Harris. I admire the work you do."

"Thanks. I've read your poems. Roz gave me one of your collections."

"Really?" I said. "Which one?"

"I think it had a blue cover. Or maybe it was orange. Or green. Was it green?"

"Doesn't matter," I said.

"Roz is at a medical appointment right now—can I give her a message?"

"I just wanted to say hello."

"I'll tell her you called."

"Is she doing all right?"

"Yes, I think she is," said Harris.

Early the next morning it was misty and humid. I went to Planet Fitness and parked next to an empty beer bottle. Inside I listened to another *Sodajerker* podcast on my headphones. The two hosts, both songwriters with strong Liverpool accents, interviewed a fast-talking writer-producer named Narada Michael Walden. I'd never heard of him, but it turned out that he'd been part of big hits for Whitney Houston and Aretha Franklin, after drumming in exotic time-signatures for the Mahavishnu Orchestra. He cowrote Jermaine Stewart's "We Don't Have to Take Our Clothes Off." He came up with Aretha Franklin's "Who's Zoomin' Who" by interviewing her on the phone. Aretha said that when she goes to a club and she sees an attractive man in the corner, she checks him out while he checks her out and she's like, "Who's zoomin' who?" That became the song.

The Sodajerkers asked Narada Michael Walden if he liked working with women. He said yes, because they're beautiful, with beautiful smiles and nice smells—but because they're divas, with precious living hearts, sometimes they call for special treatment. For instance Whitney Houston. Once Walden was working with Whitney after she and Eddie Murphy split up. He'd also produced a song with Eddie

Murphy, "Put Your Mouth on Me." So he knew Eddie. He said to Whitney Houston: "Do you want me to go beat up Eddie?" After that, he said, Whitney knew Narada really cared about her, and she sang her loving life out for him in the studio and produced jewels and diamonds of melodic elaboration.

I listened to all this on the elliptical trainer. Walden said he began as a drummer and he still thinks like one. The drummer in him, he said, brings the funk out. "Drumming is so raw. Brutal. Snot. It's a thing that happens that you can't get by playing the pretty keyboard. The people who stay popular year after year are funk people who understand rhythm." Why was that? Because people want to dance. "Even look at a chick like Barbra Streisand, who I adore," he said. She didn't have a huge pop hit till she left her Broadway singing style behind and started emphasizing the syncopation: "And we got nothing to be guil—tee—of." What Walden is always trying for is a hit. "A lot of people don't talk about that, but I will." To get a hit, he said, you have to be totally committed. "You have to put your hit hat on."

Shit, my hit hat! Forget the misery hat, where's my hit hat? I wanted one. I did a round of the upper-arm machines wanting to write a hit song called "Why Are You Fat?" I have the beginnings of an unpleasant potbelly and I hate it. You're fat, I wanted to say, because you are a lazy fat fuck. You eat bags of nut snacks that make you fat. You eat peanut butter crackers that make you fat. You sit on your donkey ass smoking Fausto cigars and drinking coffee and eating stale shortbread cookies rather than going outside and mowing the weeds or taking a walk with the dog or eating a carrot and writing a poem. You're fat because the corn in food is so ridiculously cheap, and you're too fucking lazy to read the ingredients to see that they've put twelve powdered poisons in there. And you're fat because you're morally fat. You haven't taken time to figure out what's right. You don't do enough for other people. You failed to have a child.

But at least you're not fat from taking antidepressants. Roz did a powerful show on weight gain and antidepressants. People start taking Zoloft or Paxil and they blimp out—they put on forty pounds of belly fat immediately. Plus they lose their joy in sex, and they're addicted to the pills, and if they try to go off them because they don't like being fat and want to have a few solid orgasms, they experience awful neural symptoms called "brain zaps" or "brain shivers." Ugh.

Was there a hit song there? "Brain shivers, I've got the chills. Brain shivers, can't get off the pills." Possibly, with the right bassline.

I WENT OUT to the parking lot and discovered that I'd locked my keys in the Kia. I could see them dangling below the steering wheel. That's the second time this year that I've locked myself out of my car, plus three dead-battery jumps. It's pure absentmindedness, fat-headedness, and there's no excuse for it. I called AAA and told the woman my problem.

She said, "I can help you with that." However, because I'd used up all my free service calls it would cost me forty dollars. I said I understood. She said the truck would be there in half an hour. Triple A works just the way real insurance should work, pooling many payers to help out unfortunate fools like me with their infrequent crises. Health insurance can't work like that, because, as Prince said, we're all going to die. Health insurance is doomed, because everyone is doomed and everyone can't pay for everyone's needless colonoscopy and preventive polyp removal. This and Obama's wars may bring down the government. If a collapse comes, followed by hyperinflation, we'll suffer and get thin and there won't be so many academic departments of creative writing. Please just ignore this tiresome politicizing.

I went back inside. It happened to be bagel morning at Planet Fitness, and the bagels were going fast. I love onion bagels, and everything bagels, even though it hurts my jaw to chew them. They help me think, and I was famished. I toasted an everything bagel after hacking it apart with a plastic knife, and while I was waiting for it to brown I listened to Whitney Houston sing "I Wanna Dance with Somebody." I carved out a generous wodge of cream cheese and spread it around and went outside to lean against my trunk. I chewed and listened with awe and an odd kind of patriotism to Whitney's Super Bowl performance of "The Star-Spangled Banner" while I admired the unusual Portsmouth mist. The best everything bagels come frozen from New York City, but these were quite good. What makes an everything bagel great, even better than a cigar, is the almost burned bits of onion. The crunchy, sweet, bitter bits of tiny onion asteroids taste beyond-words good. They help a lot if you've drunk too much Yukon Jack the night before, but I'm finding that they help even if you haven't. I haven't had anything to drink in more than a month and I feel great. Caramelization is the great achievement of cooking.

I sent a text to Roz. "Just hoping you're feeling okay— also sad news, Nan's mother (next-door neighbor Nan) died." Nan and Roz hadn't been close friends, but they liked each other.

The Triple A man arrived at 7:51. The radio was going in his truck before he shut off the motor. He used a technique I hadn't seen before. With a rubber bulb he inflated the gap between the door and the car and then he angled a long metal tool in. But instead of trying to get a purchase on the clicker's indentation to pry it upward, he reached farther. I thought he was going to try to open the door by pulling on the door handle, and I said, "I'm afraid this isn't a car that unlocks automatically when you pull the inside handle."

"I'm going to unroll the window," he said drily.

"That's brilliant," I said. I looked in through the window on the other side and watched the clawed chicken foot of his metal tool pushing and pulling the window handle around. It took him a long time, but eventually he got the window open enough to get his arm in, and then he pulled on the lock and opened the door.

"Fantastic," I said.

He tapped his head. "You've got to keep thinking."

He was a young kid with a beard, retro-hippie-ish but with an official AAA shirt on, recently graduated from the University of New Hampshire. I flipped open my wallet and gave him a twenty from the back of my stash, where the twenties usually hide. I couldn't afford it, but it's important to give credit where credit is due.

"What kind of songs do you listen to when you're driving?" I asked.

"The Cowboy Junkies," he said. "They've got a song called 'Common Disaster.' Also I like Ben Taylor. He's the son of James Taylor and Carly Simon."

"Thanks for telling me."

I scribbled "Common Disaster" and "Ben Taylor" on my folded-up piece of paper. Then I wrote "everything bagel" and "You've got to keep thinking"—maybe they could be songs.

Twenty-six

M Y JAW ACHES, and a drowsy numbness pains my sense. The cigar smoking is not good for it. It's not the jaw it once was, and I'll tell you what happened. In freshman year of high school, when I played basketball, I knew this kid named Ronnie who was a master dribbler. He had many tricky dribbles, but there was a certain move that worked every time—a low double-bounce feint, performed inches above the floor, that threw you off when you were trying to block his shot. I admired him very much even before we played basketball together, because of how well he drummed on his algebra textbook.

And the interesting thing about him, which I found out in gym class, was that he was missing a pectoral muscle. I don't know if he'd been born without it, or if he'd had it removed, but it wasn't there. He could drum in patterns I'd never heard before, and he could turn in the air and make a basket from half a mile away, and he did all this with only one pectoral muscle. Once he said, matter-of-factly, "Black people are just better than white people. They're better at all sports, they sing better, they climb the rope higher, they run the hurdles faster, they win at the Olympics. They're just better at everything." And I thought, He's absolutely right about that. Even so, I wanted to learn how to do his double-bounce trick.

I watched his moves carefully at practice, and then I went off to a far corner of the gym to try the double dribble. I thought I had it, or a close approximation of it, but a few days later, when I tried it in a game, I did something wrong. I bent low, feinted, double-dribbled, and the basketball came up fast and hit me in the jaw. I felt something go pop. It was extremely painful. Tears obscured my vision. Somebody grabbed the ball and I backed away from the action to recover. The pain was all over the right side of my head.

It didn't go away. At inter-high band practice on Saturday morning we were playing a piece by Vincent Persichetti and an arrangement of Santana's "Black Magic Woman." My jaw hurt too much to play, but I pretended by frowning and putting my lips loosely on the reed. It didn't matter that I wasn't making any sound—the bassoon part was doubled by the bass clarinets and the baritone saxes. At Youth Orchestra on Sunday we spent an hour on *The Pines of Rome*, by Respighi, and I faked playing there, too, saving myself for the exposed passage near the beginning of *Afternoon of a*

Faun. I had trouble eating a Ry-Krisp when I got home. I gave my jaw two days of rest, but then I had to practice a Milde étude for my lesson on Thursday.

I found out that the only way I could play the bassoon with a bearable level of pain was with my jaw positioned in a slight state of dislocation. Every day I popped my jaw gently out of alignment and practiced. I didn't tell my teacher, Bill, for a few months, and the pain gradually diminished. But there was something clearly not right in what I was doing. When I finally told him about the basketball incident, he laughed a sad, kindly laugh. "I guess that's dedication," he said. He had a flaxen-haired girlfriend who was also a flutist. I had kind of a crush on her. I think Billy knew. They played the Villa-Lobos "Bachianas Brasileiras No. 6" together—a winsome, wide-wandering duet for flute and bassoon. Once the two of them taught me how to smoke a joint. It did nothing for me.

And that's how I wrecked my jaw.

I've been working on a love song that goes, "I want to go to the beach, I want to take the dog off the leash, I want to stare out to the east, I want to see a new shade of blue, I want to smell the seaweed with you." The first melody I tried was too close to Leonard Cohen's "Hallelujah," so I rethought it. At one point I stopped singing and said, with amazement, "I'm actually writing a frigging love song."

I wish I could sing "Bachianas Brasileiras No. 5" for you. It's the famous one. "Bachianas Brasileiras No. 6" is for flute and bassoon, and only bassoonists and flutists know about it, but "Bachianas Brasileiras No. 5" was an international hit. Heitor Villa-Lobos put on his hit hat that week and produced a masterpiece that everyone should listen to when they are seeking comfort.

Just saying the composer's name is a musical experience. You need that *sh* in there: Villa-Lobosh. He was a prolific composer from where—Buenos Aires? Somewhere like that. São Paulo? Oh, *Bachianas Brasileiras*, right. He was a Brazilian composer. In nine separate short pieces, he took the example of Bach and gave it his own Brazilian bean-salad sexual curvature. And for No. 5, he used eight cellos—I think it's eight, or twelve, or fifteen, an incredible number of cellos—and one human voice.

You can think of Villa-Lobos sitting there thinking, No, I'm not going to have one cello, or two, or three, I'm going to have a whole lot of cellos. All played by beautiful dark-haired women in loose flowing skirts. And they'll all be doing pizzicato, plucking their long strings with their heads cocked to one side, *bung bung bung bung bung bung bung bung bung bung bung bung bung bung*—a pizzicato obbligato. Obliged to pluck. Pluck on, beautiful cello women! And then coming in over the mandatory pluckage is a melodic line that's like Bach but it's been run through the South American flan factory, sung by a singer named Victoria de los Angeles. My father had her record. She's some kind of full-chested contralto, or maybe she's a soprano, and she can belt it out. She goes, "Laaaaaaaaaah, daaaah daaaah daah daah dah dah daaaaaaaaah!"

Well, I can't get that high. Anyway, she sings like a mad tropical bird, and it's just a fondue of molten wanting and grieving and everything that you wish you could remember and feel and know. "Noh ooh, doo dooodoo dooooo deedoodie doooooooooooo! Dooooooo dah deee da doodie dooooooh!"

Sorry. I don't even come close. But today I looked up Victoria de los Angeles on iTunes and listened to her sing the *Bachianas* again, for the first time since I sold my bassoon. It's an old recording, all mono. I heard the same hiss, the same cellos. I could see my dear father standing between the Bose speakers, listening and moving his arms. All those cello players are dead and gone now, probably. And my father is gone, and Victoria de los Angeles is gone, and Heitor Villa-Lobos is gone now, too. He died when I was two. He wrote too much and most of his compositions are forgotten. But he did dream up this big, bad moonload of greatness for a loving voice and a bunch of cellos. When Victoria of the Angels started singing, I just lost it. It's spontaneous. It's the spontaneous overflow of powerful feelings, is what it is. All carefully written down as notes.

I ANSWERED THE PHONE. "Hi," said Roz.

"Hi! Just a sec, let me turn this down." I was listening to

"You Dropped a Bomb on Me" at high volume. "How are you making out?"

"Well, so I'm having it done tomorrow."

"You're kidding. That's so soon."

"I know. They had an opening at the hospital and the doctor says one of my ovaries is at risk, and I kind of like my ovaries."

"Me, too."

"So, it's tomorrow."

"Can I be there—or—"

"Lucy's driving to the hospital with me, and Harris says he's going to try to be there as well—so it might be difficult."

"Oh. Hm. Well, what are you doing right now?"

"Nothing," Roz said. "I'm not supposed to eat anything, so I'm just sitting here staring at a tub of sesame seeds."

"That doesn't sound like much fun."

"No, and the idea of them feeling around in my innards tomorrow disgusts me. Those gloved groping hands, ugh. I hate surgery."

"Should I come over and fluff you up?"

"I'm in my pajamas and I'm not going to be much fun. On the other hand, tomorrow's really impossible, and I don't want you to think that you're not part of it, because you are. You really are."

"Then why don't I drive over and see you right now? We can watch a movie. I rented the Talking Heads movie, *Stop Making Sense*. I've never seen it. I don't believe you've seen it, have you?"

"No, I haven't."

"Well then, what do you think? We can have a pre-op viewing of the Talking Heads. I think they wear enormous suits with huge shoulders. It's directed by Jonathan Demme. It's supposed to be good. We can watch people in huge business suits singing 'Take Me to the River' and forget about our troubles."

Roz chuckled. "That sounds kind of good. Bring your pajamas and we can have a pajama party. And can you bring the dear dog?"

"He'd love to see you."

"Good, then come over."

Twenty-seven

I SHOWERED OFF the day's cigar smell and found a fairly
clean pair of pajama bottoms, and Smacko and I drove
at a good clip to Roz's condo in Concord, which is easy to
spot because on the steps up to her door are many small
mossy pots. Roz offered both of us seats on the couch—idly
I tweaked the piping on the armrest while she smelled the
dog's paws, as she liked to do. She was wearing a light
bathrobe and pajamas and fluffy slippers. She asked me how
my music was going.

"Going fine, going well," I said.

"Can I hear some songs?"

"I'm still fiddling with them. I put some marimba trills in
one of the songs. It's for you. Actually, several of them are for
you. I'll burn you a CD when they're done."

"Marimba trills. How nice."

Roz had popped some popcorn, but she said she couldn't

have any. Then she relented. "Oh, heck, I'll have two pieces. They won't kill me, and I'm starving." She crunched defiantly.

We started the DVD. It was a concert movie and David Byrne looked completely insane. He had no stage patter. He began singing "Psycho Killer" on a bare stage, with his guitar and a drum loop. I didn't like it much. I glanced at Roz. She looked doubtful.

"Hm," I said, "shall we skip ahead?"

"Maybe."

We skipped through several songs. "Slippery People" was a bit of a disappointment—more of the musicians were on the stage, including two backup singers who helped a lot, but it didn't sound as good as the recorded version, with Tina Weymouth playing her clean thumpity-funk bass. There wasn't much humanity in what David Byrne was doing. It was all too arty, too knowingly ironic. Maybe at a different time I would have liked it, but it definitely wasn't the sort of thing to watch if you were with a person who was having a hysterectomy the next morning.

"I really don't know what to say," I said. "Let me see if I can find 'Take Me to the River.'"

"Okay."

I skipped to the end, where they all did an extended version of "Take Me to the River." It was good. They were sweating now, and the beat was phenomenal, and a percussionist named Steve Scales was malleting away on an array of gourds, and the audience helped them with the chorus. I looked over at Roz, who was rocking, to my immense relief. The Talking Heads had come alive, and it was pure river-bathing genius. Even David Byrne was smiling, finally.

When it was over the audience went wild and the Talking Heads did an encore, which we fast-forwarded through. The stage crew, in black, filed across the stage, and he thanked them. The credits came on. Fifteen minutes had elapsed for Roz and me.

"Well, well, well," said Roz. "All you need is one great song."

"It's true," I said.

We were a little at a loss. "This was fun," said Roz.

I flung a piece of popcorn to Smack, who caught it in his mouth. "No, it wasn't," I said. "Shit. I wanted to make you feel better. I don't want to be a person who plays 'Psycho Killer' to his lifelong friend before her operation."

"That's okay."

"What kind of movie would you really like to see right now? What's your very favorite movie these days?"

Roz said that honestly her favorite film of all time was *The Philadelphia Story*. "But I know you have a prejudice against black-and-white movies."

"No, I'm different now. I'm broadening my horizons. I've never seen it."

"It's a marvelous comedy. Katharine Hepburn is tremendous."

"If it's your favorite movie, then we should watch it right now."

AND THAT'S what we did. We watched *The Philadelphia Story*. Roz found it on Netflix. We were transfixed. We laughed and we cried. It was two hours of total delight. Jimmy Stewart and Katharine Hepburn and Cary Grant were all brilliant, and so was the younger sister in her ballet slippers. Halfway through, Roz put her head on my shoulder like the old days.

"Now that's a movie," I said.

"It is," said Roz. "Thank you for watching it with me. Phew! I feel better."

"I'm glad. I—" I trailed off. "I don't want to overload you with gobs of raw emotion."

"Oh, don't worry about that. I could use some raw emotion. Harris's bedside manner has been a little lacking. He's being chilly about all this."

"He is, is he? Why are you dating this awful man?"

Roz thought about this for a moment. "Because I admire his courage. He says things that make his colleagues very angry at him, but I think he's right a lot of the time. And he's funny and smart, and attractive."

I grunted.

"And he courted me and fussed over me, and that felt really good," Roz said. "But he's being strange about the surgery. I think he's disappointed in me for needing a hysterectomy. There were so many hysterectomies done in the past, unnecessarily—it's a real scandal—and he's been such an opponent of that. And now here I am going under the knife."

"But that's life," I said. "That's the way life is."

"I guess so. Maybe we shouldn't talk about Harris."

"Okay, well—I just want to say I love you very much, whatever my legal status is, ex-boyfriend, jilted lover, picnic partner, future husband, whatever."

"Husband, whoa, whoa. *Philadelphia Story* really did a job on you. But I love you, too, Pauly. I'm scared. I don't like anesthesia. I'm really scared."

"I know you are, but it's going to be okay," I said. "You're doing what you need to do, and you're going to be fine." Roz looked like she was beginning to droop. I said, "Should I go back now so you can get some rest, or should I sleep on the couch?"

"Cary Grant would probably sleep on the couch," she said. "Lucy's picking me up at six a.m."

"Boy, they start early at hospitals."

Roz went off to get a pillow and a blanket. When she handed them to me, she said, shyly, "Do you still want to feel my fibroid?"

"Yes, if you want me to."

She sat back down next to me. "I think I do. Anyway, this is your last chance. It won't be there tomorrow." She took my hand and placed it on her stomach.

"Hm," I said. "I definitely feel something hard and knotted, but I think it's your bathrobe. You know, the sash."

"Oh, it's lower down than that." She undid her bathrobe. Her pajamas had narrow light blue stripes.

I touched her warm, soft, private pajamas and now I could definitely feel it. I held my hand there for a moment. "I feel it," I said. I felt a sadness and took my hand away. "So that's it."

"That's what's causing all the trouble," she said. "What a word, 'fibroid.'"

"Sounds like a new kind of cellphone."

"The Verizon Fibroid," she said. "With an unlimited monthly data plan."

I laughed. "I sure wish this didn't have to happen to you."

"But it does," Roz said. "It's bleeding me white. It's got to go. Thanks for the molasses, by the way—it helped."

"I'd like to be at the hospital tomorrow," I said.

"No, please, it's just too complicated. Lucy will be with me. I'll be very out of it, anyway. We'll talk afterward. Thank you for coming over. It was very nice of you."

"I'm going to buy you a canoe," I said. "I really am." I cleared my throat. "Can I, uh, ask a rude question? What does your doctor say about marital relations afterward—is it all, you know, Tyrconnell and pussy licking and hand jobs?"

"My doctor assures me that everything will work fine afterward. In fact, she claims that sex will be better. My cervix will still be in place."

I threw my hands up. "Ah, your cervix will be in place!"

"You wicked man." Roz smiled at me. "Good night, sweetie."

Smack trotted behind Roz into her bedroom and I slept on the couch. I left at five-thirty the next morning—Roz was nervous and hungry and seemed to want to avoid having to explain my presence to Lucy, which I understood. I drove home and sprinkled some cracked corn for Nan's chickens.

Twenty-eight

I SANG MYSELF HOARSE THIS MORNING, working for two hours on the harmonies in "Marry Me." I had that strange mental clarity you get sometimes when you haven't had a shower and you haven't had enough sleep. Right now it's noon and very hot and I'm parked in a bit of shade at the edge of the hospital parking lot. Roz is probably in surgery at this moment. This is awful. The only thing I can compare this to is scenes in old movies where men are waiting to hear that their wife has had a baby. But we're not having a baby. That's just the way it is.

You hear a lot about the poet's voice. Swinburne's voice as opposed to Wallace Stevens's voice, as opposed to Hopkins's voice, as opposed to, say, Tony Hoagland's voice. There's an anthology called *The Voice of the Sea*, filled with sea poems. But what does it mean to say you have a voice when you're a poet? When you have deliberately melted away your voice, and you're left with nothing but the wire armature? All the wax, all the bones and muscle of the sound, are gone. There's a moment in *The Fly*, David Cronenberg's movie, toward the end, where the big humanoid fly squirts some acid on a man's arm. It burns away the man's arm down to the bone.

That's what happens when you write down a sentence, or a stanza. When you think of it, you imagine it in all its fleshed-out, full-voiced spoken plenitude. It's a fat, healthy living thing that comes out of a throat, made up of movements of tongue and mouth and jaw. And tiny meetings of flesh. The little vagina in the throat clenches, and air comes pushing up through it, and oooh! There it goes, up into the mouth, where it's manipulated by the lips and tongue, the way a balloon is twisted into funny shapes by a clown at a children's birthday party.

So it comes into being as an audible phrase, as a living heavy healthy plump fleshy thing. For instance, Yeats: "Oh cruel death, give three things back / Sang a bone upon the shore." And then a strange thing happens that the poet does, and I'm not sure it's a good thing. The poet says, No, thanks, I don't want the flesh, I want the bones. I want only the words. Because there's this nifty notation system that we've developed, and it's quite sophisticated. It uses twenty-six symbols, and those symbols are able to record each word that I'm speaking, and even to record, in a crude way, with the help of commas and semicolons and periods, some of the nuances of the pauses between my words. So I'm going to roll it all out as bones. I'm going to take this living thing and I'm going to render it, boil it down. Once there was sound, and now there are words on a page.

So then you publish your poem, all boiled down, all white bones. And readers come along years later and say that the interesting thing about so-and-so's "voice" is X. Even though they may never have heard the poet's voice. What they've done is they have extrapolated. They've supplied their own guesses about how a person like this poet would speak, and they have managed to reclothe, or reincarnate, that printed skeleton in flesh. And of course I'm fine with that. It has to happen, and there are good things about it because the eye is a bullet train and can read quickly. It's easier to read with the eye than to listen to somebody speak. But there are also losses, because your reconstruction of the poet's voice may be all wrong.

An anthropologist will take a few surviving pieces of a Neanderthal's skull—a cheekbone and a bit of jawbone—and he'll build out a whole skull from that, and he'll use modeling clay to flesh out the extrapolated skull with sinews and muscles and cheeks, and when he's done he thinks he is looking at the face of a Neanderthal. He doesn't know if he's right. He thinks he is. We want to believe him. But he's never seen a Neanderthal.

He could be completely wrong. If you go to Planet Fitness and study the differences in the way flesh hangs off people's bodies, you know that he is almost certainly somewhat wrong. Was it a fat Neanderthal? Or "Neandertal," with a hard *t*? There's no way to know. Presumably there were a few overweight Neanderthals. All it takes is some dead mammoths at the foot of a cliff and an interest in eating.

So there are losses incurred when you go from the spoken universe of sound envelopes that start and stop and die away, that can be looked at on an oscilloscope, to this whole other universe, which is hooks and eyes of code on some sort of page or screen. The page or screen is white, and the shapes on it are black—or vice versa, if you invert the colors for night reading, as I do. We learned to read the code sometime around the age of six, and we're pretty good at it, and eventually we stop moving our lips. We think of the denatured words as the distillation of everything essential. We embrace the denaturing, and we develop prose styles that are so conventionalized, so depersonalized, that they fit well with the fact that all the sound flesh has been melted off.

Take the journalistic style of *The New York Times*, on its front page. It uses stock phrases like "said yesterday," and you really can't tell one writer from another. If you talked to each of the reporters who wrote articles for the front page, you'd realize immediately that they are very different, intelligent people. Some of them you'd like quite a lot, and some of them you might like less. You would know a great deal about them, if you talked to each of them for a minute, or if you heard them explaining what they were writing about in their articles. All that voicedness is gone—each of their "today"s is exactly the same. Everyone says "today" or "yesterday" the same on the page, because it is the same number of letters, the same typestyle. And yet each of those reporters says "yesterday," and understands yesterday, differently. There are a thousand different ways to say "hello," but there's only one way to say it in print. That's what we're losing.

And that's what music is all about. Music is about the idea that one cellist's A is going to sound slightly different from another cellist's A, and if you have six or seven or twelve cellos in a row, they're going to sound different from six trombones in a row. Donald Sutherland used to do the voiceovers for Volvo commercials. We never saw his face, but we knew it was Sutherland—he said "airbags" differently from anyone else. Marvin Gaye sings "ooh" differently from the way Keri Noble sings "ooh." Paul McCartney's "Yesterday" is very different from Boyz II Men's "Yesterday." My "Marry me" is different from Cary Grant's "Marry me."

AT FOUR I SAW LUCY leave from the main exit with Harris—I was certain it was Harris because I'd studied his picture on the *Medicine Ball* website. He was smiling. The two of them shook hands and drove away in separate cars. My cellphone plinked. It was Lucy. "Everything went well," she said. "She's very groggy but she's doing fine. She's sleeping now."

"Oh good, that's good, that's good," I said. I took a deep breath and drove to RiverRun Books—they've relocated to a smaller space—and bought a copy of Mary Oliver's *New and Selected Poems, Volume Two* to give to Roz when she got home. A woman who works there runs a blog called *Write*

Place, Write Time where writers send in photographs of their work areas and describe them. I keep hoping she'll ask me to contribute so that I can take a picture of my car, but she hasn't yet.

I ordered the Enchiladas Banderas at Margarita's—no meat in honor of Roz—and then I went to Planet Fitness. On the way home I was stopped by a cop because I didn't use my left-turn signal at a deserted intersection. His siren yipped once and I saw the flashing. I whispered, "What the fuck did I do? What, you dick-fucking shitasser?"

I heard a door thump closed. I put on my hazard lights and unrolled the window all the way. I considered hurriedly wiping my face, so I wouldn't look sweaty, but thought it might seem suspicious.

"Do you know why I stopped you?" the cop said, shining a flashlight.

"No," I said. The cop was about twenty-three, trying to be authoritative and professional. Newly trained.

He said, "You didn't signal when you turned left. Also you were driving slowly."

"Oh gee, I'm sorry, Officer."

"Have you been drinking?"

"No, not recently."

"Please get out of the car."

The cop offered me a seat on his front bumper, where there was a little black ledge, and he spent a while checking my license and registration. Then he came out holding a ballpoint pen. He pointed his flashlight at my face and moved the ballpoint pen back and forth. "I'm going to ask you to keep your head still and follow the tip of the pen with your eyes," he said.

I watched the ballpoint go back and forth, sometimes eclipsing the flashlight. It was a Pilot G-2 fine-point pen. I felt shifty, like the corner-glancing cherub in the Christmas card.

"That's the kind of pen I use," I said.

"Hm," he said.

He moved the pen way over to the left and I strained to follow it. My eyeballs wobbled. "You're exceeding the limits of my vision," I said. "I feel like Richard Nixon at the optometrist."

"I know, that's how it works," he said. "Are you sure you haven't been drinking?"

"Yes, I'm sure. I would remember. I spent most of today at the hospital. A friend of mine just had a hysterectomy."

"Is she all right?"

"Yes, she is." He passed the pen back and forth again, and then he gave me a long look. "You can go back to your car now." I got up and he walked with me. He said, "Can you please tell me why you have a bottle of beer near your seat?"

"What bottle of beer?" I said, puzzled. I opened the door and saw what he'd seen. "It's Pellegrino," I said, pulling it out. "Sparkling water. I drink it after I go to Planet Fitness."

"All right," he said, shining his flashlight on it. He handed me a ticket. "I'm giving you a warning for making a left turn without signaling."

"Okay, thanks, sorry."

"Have a good evening, and remember your turn signals. People need to know where you're going."

"I will. Thanks again."

I drove away. I lit a Fausto, puffed it, and cackled.

Twenty-nine

I'VE TALKED TO LUCY—who has, by the way, red hair and a faint midwestern accent. Roz is home from the hospital and she's sleeping a lot. I'm going to call her tomorrow to say hello.

I spent all afternoon playing Logic's Steinway Hall Piano. I didn't use any other instruments. By playing slowly and then speeding it up, and by adding one line over another, I could sound a little like Glenn Gould, which is a powerful feeling. After that I experimented with some slow ninth chords, and I got something going that I liked, and I put some words to the chords: "I saw you / I heard your voice / And then one day I knew / I loved you." Another love song. At around noon, the Axiom keyboard developed a problem: Middle C wouldn't play. I looked up "Axiom silent key" on some discussion forums. Apparently it's a known problem. There's a loose connection somewhere, and a key, often middle C, will just stop speaking. This is frustrating if you're trying to compose a piece of music with a middle C. I thought I was going to have to drive back to Best Buy and return the keyboard. Then I found a video in which someone posted a solution: You squeeze hard on the two sides of the plastic near the mod wheel. I tried it and it worked perfectly. I'm overjoyed, because I really like this keyboard. Just give it a squeeze.

Glenn Gould, you know, used to sing along while he played Bach. He was a hero of mine when I was in high school. I liked his clean staccato playing style. Later, when I got into Debussy's *Preludes* and Grieg's *Lyric Pieces*, I was less sure about him. He wrote a fugue called "So You Want to Write a Fugue." It's got a funny title and good lyrics, but it isn't all that original a piece of music. Gould was a performer, not a creator. He was cold all the time. He took pills and he wore scarves and hats and coats indoors. The film about him, *Thirty Two Short Films About Glenn Gould*, begins with him standing on a windswept ice field. What was missing from Gould's art was very simple: love. His jumpy playing style showed that—or no, that's a cheap shot. He sat very low in front of the piano and did beautiful things to it.

Nowadays for Bach's keyboard music I like a pianist named András Schiff. He's also a bit of an eccentric, but he has a much more legato playing style—"legato" means "tied together." One note hands things off in a bucket brigade to the next. Schiff doesn't believe in scales and Czerny études. He practices every day by playing the music he actually likes, for instance Bach's two-part inventions. He's a believer in silences. He said in an interview that when he gives a concert, he sometimes wishes that nobody would applaud. Play it, finish it, and let the music's close contrapuntal reasoning live on for a while in the audience's mind. Some of his Bach recordings begin with an unusually long silence.

You never applaud or say "Amen" after someone's spoken in Quaker meeting. You're not supposed to compliment someone after meeting is over, either. You're not supposed to say, "I liked your message," although it's a very human urge and people do it. I did it myself after a woman talked about seeing two sparrows frolicking in her birdbath. She said she looked away and then looked back and there in place of the sparrows was a huge wild turkey. She talked about surprise and wild turkeys. Afterward, I said to her, "I liked your message."

And now I want to show you a book. Here it is. It's a novel by Theodore Dreiser called *The Genius*. I have not read it. It's Roz's book. I saw her—I heard her voice—and then one day I knew I loved her. I've never been able to read novels the way she does, though. I get about three pages in and I say, Where's my Merwin? Where's my Kunitz? Where's my Debussy? I can happily read memoirs or diaries or collections of letters, but not novels. Roz has read hundreds of novels. It didn't bother her that I didn't read them, but maybe I should have tried.

I'm going to open this book. I'm going to pick a page at random, and I'm going to read a sentence. Here we go: "He wore an old hat which he had found in a closet at Mrs. Hibberdell's, a faded, crumpled memory of a soft tan-colored sombrero which he punched jauntily to a peak and wore over one ear." Page 330. Of *The Genius* by Theodore Dreiser. Thank you. That is all.

"Hi, sweetie," said Roz, when I called. Her voice was soft and perfect—one hundred percent Roz. I could hear her smiling. She said she was doing better. "They sent me home with Vicodin and it gave me some very lurid dreams and made me forget to breathe, so I'm not taking it anymore. The pain came back, but it's bearable and better than the not breathing. Lucy's taking very good care of me."

"Good. When can I come see you?"

"Give me a few days. I need the fog to clear."

"Take it very easy," I said.

"I am," she said. "It's so nice not to think about the show. They've got a new person who's covering for me."

"That's good."

"I'm going to sleep now."

"Okay."

It's been hot and dry this week, and I thought it was time to set up the traveling sprinkler and water Nan's tomatoes. I stood watching it chuff in its slow and steady tractorish way around her tomatoes as the chickens pecked under some rhubarb leaves, unconcerned about the strange Sears machine in their garden. I'd bought an extra hose at a garage sale—better that than anger the yellowjackets. The sprinkler sprays in steady sixteenth notes. You can whistle Rossini to it if you want. Maybe I should tell you more about it.

The traveling sprinkler is a heavy metal slow-motion techno-dance-trance device with two white cast-iron toothed rear wheels that dig into the turf, and a sort of baton or helicopter blade on top that spins. The hose screws in at the back. The hose water flows at full pressure into the tractor's anus, or rectum. Up through the tractor the water goes and out the little holes at the end of the spinning whirlies, flying in a glittering bagel of sinusoidal shapes out over the garden. From certain angles it makes a close-range rainbow, and that's all very nice. But here's where the wizard mind of the innovator comes in: The spinning rotates a central post fitted with a helical thread, or worm gear, that engages with the sprockets of a driving gear that pulls two floppy hooking levers forward against the teeth on the rear wheels. First one lever pulls the right wheel forward an inch, and then the other lever pulls the left wheel forward an inch, and in that way the tractor alternatingly propels itself slowly forward, like some sort of very deliberate water clock—or like Stanley Kunitz's tortoise, "ancient and crusty, more lonely than Bonaparte."

But that isn't the really beautiful part of this invention, this three-part invention that Bach would have loved to water his Lutheran tomatoes with. The beautiful part comes in front, where there is a small, seemingly atrophied wheel. This wheel is curved so that it can fit over the hose. Thus the tractor, as it moves along, is compelled to follow the route of its own motive force. The hose becomes the guidance system. Consider for a moment the power and the glory of that.

You may say, well, obviously it's propelled by water, and obviously it follows the hose. But it wasn't so obvious in 1909, when Benjamin Sweney got a patent for his sprinkler. Sweney's sprinkler sprinkled and moved forward at the same time, but it didn't do anything with the hose except drag it behind. Not enough. Viggo Nielsen, an Australian, got his tractor sprinkler patent in 1933. It sprinkled and moved and it rolled the hose up on itself. Not quite right, either. Then came a Nebraskan freethinker, John Wilson. Wilson got two water sprinkler patents. His first sprinkler looked like an old-fashioned bicycle, with a large wheel in front and a small wheel in back. The large wheel was a gear, pushed by a pawl—a word later made famous by Richard Eberhart, in his poem "The Fury of Aerial Bombardment." But Wilson wasn't satisfied. The second patent, applied for in September 1941, was for a sprinkler that looked the way the traveling sprinkler looks now. That's when it all came together. Just before World War II, Wilson disassembled a piece of dairy equipment called a cream separator and used a piece from it as the driving gear in the middle of his machine, while in front he put a small loose wheel that wanted to go wherever the hose went. Now the source of the sprinkler's power was the route it took: the link back to its past was also its future. You could buy more hose and make long twisty routes for it to follow, even up slight grades if you wanted. As long as you didn't set the hose up so that there was too sharp a turn, the sprinkler would go anywhere. It was the trustiest little hardworking machine. And if you got tired of watching it, and went inside after a while, as I used to do, to make a sandwich, the tractor, this Great American Invention, would finally arrive at the moment when the two universes of forward and backward time would collide at the faucet by the house.

National Walking Sprinkler of Nebraska made Wilson's machines, and they still do. They made them for Sears and that's where my father bought his. Everything about it is immediately understandable. It's what America did before it threw itself wholeheartedly into the making of weapons that kill everyone.

I have been trying to write a poem about this sprinkler for years, because I like it so much, and I've never managed to do it. What a joy now to wind it around Nan's tomatoes and watch it, in all its intuitive clumsy ungainly beauty, do some good.

RAYMOND TURNED in the driveway while I was standing watching the sprinkler. "Hey, hey," he said. "That's a handy little machine."

"Isn't it? I don't often get a chance to use it. I'm terribly sorry about your grandmother."

"Oh, thanks. It's very sad."

"How's your mother doing?"

"She's okay, I think."

We looked at the sprinkler twirl. I asked him how his music was progressing.

"I've got a new song," he said.

"Can I hear it?"

We went up to his room, which had a poster of Bob Marley on the wall and a corner filled with a multileveled shrine of musical machinery. There were two important-looking squarish studio speakers with yellow cones. Raymond played me his new track, called "Promises Burn." He played it loud, but even so I couldn't make out all the lyrics, which went by fast. I heard the chorus, though: "Lips say words and promises burn, so can we." It was a genuine brainworm, and I said so. I suspected that Raymond had been through some recent unhappiness with his girlfriend, but we didn't talk about it. He showed me how he'd used three vocoder tracks to mix pitched synthesizer sounds in with his singing, and he revealed a neat trick for reversing a piano note using a virtual guitar pedal, so that it plays backward: yeet, yeet, yit!

"There's so much to this software," I said, shaking my head. I told him I'd been working on some dance songs, but they weren't finished. "If you ever want to try making a song together, just let me know."

"Sure," Raymond said. "You could email me some chords and I could email you some beats and we'll each work on what the other person began. How about that?"

I said that sounded good.

"If we end up with something usable, I'll play it at Stripe.

I'm guest DJ'ing there next week. I'm going to drop some Diplo on them. 'Shake it till it pops out.'"

"That sounds great. What's Stripe?"

"It's a dance club. It's on Chapel Street."

"Oh, okay," I said. Suddenly I remembered Nan's tomatoes. "Shoot, I better go check the sprinkler now."

I went outside. My tractor had made almost the full circuit around the tomato bed. The chickens were flapping their wings just out of range of the spray. The rooster crowed.

Thirty

I'M DRIVING HOME NOW from Federal Cigar with all the windows open and the air shuddering through the car, and as you can see it's one of those days in which visual beauty has been laid on—lain on?—has been laid on with a trowel. There was a new man at Federal Cigar, a serious chap with a zip-up vest. I asked him to recommend some cigars that were like Faustos but different. "I might try the Skull Breaker," he said. "Or the Bone Crusher." I bought both of them—they were cheaper than the others—plus eight Faustos and a fourteen-dollar top-shelf creation with a pointy tip. This could get expensive. On impulse I drove down Chapel Street past the gray-and-pink-striped door that leads into Stripe, the dance club that Raymond told me about. I had a moment of thrilled apprehension. It's not really for fifty-five-year-olds, I don't think. I've hardly ever been to a dance club. Even back when I was writing dirty poems I was more of a dance-at-home kind of guy. I had some good twirly moves, though.

I just listened to Cormac McCarthy—not the novelist, the musician—sing one of his songs, "Light at the Top of the Stairs." He's got a voice that can do everything. I met him once. He lives near here. He writes songs that tell whole stories, the way Pat Pattison wants us to. He plays at the Press Room sometimes. I'm jealous of him.

I'm going to park and try a Bone Crusher. I'll save the Skull Breaker for later.

AMY LOWELL, queen of the Imagist poets, said that you prepare a cigar for smoking the way you seduce a woman. First you unwrap its tinfoil wrapper. That's like removing her dress. Then you take off the label—that's like the shift. Finally you're down to the nude cigar. Amy Lowell would have enjoyed smoking this Bone Crusher. It's true to its name, good gracious.

Archibald MacLeish paid court to Amy Lowell in Paris. He was an assiduous suckup—he wrote her, "I have even seen your long library in my dreams, & in my so-called waking hours I spend hours there"—and with Lowell's help he got Harriet Monroe to publish some of his poems in *Poetry*. Then later, when he'd become a hotshot Pulitzer man and had fallen under the spell of Eliot's *Waste Land* and Hemingway's marlin fishing, he dismissed Amy Lowell as a self-publicizer who wrote tinkly verse. And then came the

CIA, which began rewarding Jackson Pollock for painting meaningless paintings. Nicolas Nabokov, a minor composer who was a friend of MacLeish's, was the CIA's liaison with the musical world. Nabokov used the CIA's money to fly the entire Boston Symphony Orchestra to Paris—in the company of crateloads of abstract paintings—where the orchestra performed *The Rite of Spring* and other advanced works, to prove that American democracy was more hip than Communism.

The Cigar Inspector has a long and thoughtful review of the Bone Crusher. I've just read it on my phone. The Cigar Inspector loves it. He wrote that initially he'd assumed it was a descendant of a memorable Viaje limited-edition cigar called the Skull and Bones, but it isn't. It's made from Nicaraguan weed, grown in volcanic Nicaraguan soil and wrapped in a broadleaf wrapper raised in the wilds of Connecticut. "It starts out pretty tame," he says, "with its power kicking in near the end." The power kicked in for me about halfway through. Wowsers. Shit on a Popsicle.

Terrible things happened in Nicaragua when Oliver North sold drugs and weapons for the CIA and used the money to fund the Nicaraguan contras, with Reagan's blessing. Thousands of people, including many children, were massacred in the fighting in the highlands near Esteli, where the good tobacco grows. Once the CIA stopped arming and training the contras, the country calmed down. Now it makes many good cigars, including the Bone Crusher. Peace reigns.

I have a strong craving to read a book that doesn't exist, called *The Manic Factor*, which diagnoses the heads of corporations who buy up lots of companies, one after another, as men in the grip of straightforward manic sprees. They're people for whom normal human spending levels are insufficient. They want to go to the big corporate tent sale and spend in the millions or billions per purchase. They don't care that they're accumulating an enormous debt, because they're manic.

I want to read a book or an article in which someone goes around and talks to board members and people in the investment business, and psychiatrists, and tells the whole story of each of these corporate self-destructions from the point of view of the buying high of their leaders. Maybe it's been done—probably it has been done, and I'll never know it because I don't read business books, or even *Forbes*.

Mania is the best way to explain the CIA, too. The manic high of knowing that you can change the history of a country by selling crack and arranging killings and handing out weapons like peanuts, all the while calling it "intelligence."

I'm eating Planter's trail mix and I'm not killing anyone. Like most people, I live my life and don't have any interest in spending secret government money trying to overthrow inconvenient regimes. I like this trail mix, although it's a little too heavy on the peanuts. We have to forgive Planter's for that—they're a peanut company, after all. The peanut guy with a monocle and spats. But the peanut taste is, to the tongue, a cliché. What you want from a trail mix are tastes that are a little less familiar—more cashews, more dried pineapple, maybe some almonds. I don't like raw peanuts, frankly—they make me feel slightly sick. Peanut butter crackers are a whole different ball game, though.

AT QUAKER MEETING the clock ticked for thirty minutes before anyone spoke. Then the wild-turkey woman got up. She said that before meeting she was out near her well, at about eight-thirty, when she saw about seventy goldfinches clinging to tall weeds with many yellow flowers. She didn't know what kind of weeds they were, but they were very tall, maybe seven feet tall. She wanted to tell us about them. There were long spider filaments stretching between them, shining in the sun, she said, and fleabane flowers below them that had still not opened for the day, and then in among the yellow weed flowers were all the marvelous goldfinches, which looked like things you'd find in cages, but they weren't caged. They were just there because they chose to be there.

Twenty minutes of silence followed. Everyone in the room was thinking about birds and weeds and the color yellow, but nobody spoke. I listened to the clock ticking, and suddenly I wanted to tell them about the click track in Paul McCartney's "Blackbird." Gabe, who volunteers at the prison, shifted in his seat and cleared his throat. I thought he was going to speak, but he didn't. It's a little like *To Tell the Truth*, the old game show, in which the contestants had to guess which of three guests was not an impostor, and at the moment of revelation one of the impostors would pretend to start to get up but then wouldn't. I began to feel the nervous fluttery feeling that meant I was going to have to say something. Finally I stood and got my balance and said that I'd heard my next-door neighbor sing the Beatles song "Blackbird" recently, and that I'd been struck by how perfect and simple a song it was, and then I'd listened to Paul McCartney sing it. It was about a man who hears a broken-winged blackbird singing at night, I said, and it's a very short song, as all the Beatles' songs were back then—just a guitar and Paul's singing. Except for one unusual thing. In addition to the music of the song, the Beatles included the click track, which is a private audio track that plays metronome clicks that the musician can hear on his headphones, so that he can keep to the beat. Normally the click track was removed in the final mix of the song, I said, but here they seem to have left it in, and in that way the song became the blackbird of itself. Its wings were broken—i.e., folded—and then comes the moment it's been waiting for, and it takes off and flies through the night forest, which is silent except for the click track of the trees. I said, "The bird has to negotiate, singingly, syncopatedly, around the trees—not hitting them, obviously—and learn to fly given the steady beat, the clock, the click track of what he's been given. We have something small and broken and we just have to wait for the right moment and make something of it and allow it to fly, and that's what Paul McCartney did, and did for us." I sat down, feeling shaky and stupid because the end was too pat. There was more silence, and then meeting ended, and everyone shook hands.

Donna said, "Thank you for choosing to come here today." There was a visitor from Saratoga, New York, who introduced herself. We said, "Welcome." There were announcements. And then the wooden wall came up and I dropped a twenty in the wicker donation basket. The woman from Eliot, Maine, was there, and she said to me, "I used to listen to my parents' record of 'Blackbird' over and over. You forgot to mention my favorite part, though. He says, 'Into the light of the dark black night.'"

I drove home thinking, That's true, that's the best thing about the song. Singing into the lit blackness of Tennyson's black-bat night, when suddenly his voice goes high and gives it a bluesy turn that is astounding. He meaning Paul, or Sir Paul as he is called now, and why not? Better that Paul McCartney is knighted than some petroleum baron or air marshal.

Thirty-one

I MAILED ROZ THE BOOK of Mary Oliver's poems and a CD with some music on it. I was going to include some of my own songs, but I thought better of it. I sent her "Bachianas Brasileiras No. 5," plus Kate Earl's "Melody," Tracy Chapman's "Change," McCartney's "Blackbird" in case she didn't have it, George Clinton's "Atomic Dog," Lennon's "Imagine," DNA's remix of Suzanne Vega's "Tom's Diner," and also, what the hell, Paul Jacobs playing Debussy's "Sunken Cathedral." I've got "The Sunken Cathedral" coming into my headphones right now. I'm listening to it all the way through for the first time since I began writing this book, if it is in fact a book, and I think it is. You have to be careful not to overlisten to a piece of music you love, or you'll wear it out—it has to last your whole life. You know it's there—the weight of the piano is there—but sometimes it's backstage, covered in quilted padding, waiting for the tuner to arrive and tighten its screws.

I have eight different versions of "The Sunken Cathedral" on iTunes. One version is played by Håkon Austbø—moody and sonorous. One is by Ingrid Fuzjko Hemming—interestingly murky, with good swinging bell-clanging. One is by Elaine Greenfield—brisker and lighter, performed on a 1907 Blüthner grand piano very similar to the one that Debussy owned. One is by Julian Lawrence Gargiulo—a live performance, with a distant energetic piano and audible chair creaks from a fidgeter nearby. One is by Arturo Benedetti Michelangeli—part of the BBC Legends series, with a wrong note enshrined in it two minutes from the beginning. One is by Noriko Ogawa—full of nervous, restrained brilliance and unusual tempos. One is by Claude Debussy himself, playing distantly on a Welte-Mignon player piano in 1914. But my favorite version is by Paul Jacobs, the pianist for the New York Philharmonic, who died of AIDS in 1983. The microphone seems to be right inside Jacobs's piano. That's the version I'm listening to now. It's so closely miked that when you swim into the center of the cathedral about halfway through and look around, the chords are almost unbearably loud—and at the end, when everything's much softer, and mortality has been faced and accepted, you can hear the felt pads come gently down to dampen the strings as they ring out their last sound.

This piece was Debussy saying good-bye to everything. It isn't specifically about the lost cathedral city of Ys, off the coast of Brittany, possibly near Douarnenez. That's a crude, programmatic interpretation that was imposed on the music after the fact by a young critic named Dane Rudhyar and an older pianist named Alfred Cortot, neither of whom knew Debussy well or understood the way his imagination worked. Saying that "The Sunken Cathedral" is about the sunken city of Ys is like saying that "Footsteps in the Snow" is about the Abominable Snowman. It's true that there is an opera by Édouard Lalo called *The King of Ys* about the flooding of Ys, based partly on a forged Breton ballad by Théodore Hersart de la Villemarqué, and true that Debussy had wildly applauded Lalo's ballet *Namouna* while at the conservatory, and had memorized parts of it, including perhaps the scandalous waltz in which Namouna rolls a cigarette for her paramour—but he was less fond of Lalo's son, Pierre, who became a powerful and malicious music critic for *Le Temps*, writing, of Debussy's *La Mer*, "I neither hear, nor see, nor feel the sea." "The Sunken Cathedral" is bigger and blurrier, more overdetermined, than the story of Ys. It's really about all sunken frightening beautiful artful ruined human things. It's about Poe's city in the sea, and about the cathedral cliffs in Tennyson's "Sea Dreams," and about the sinking cathedral and the rising lake in Rimbaud's *Illuminations*, and about the real flood of the Seine in 1910 that submerged a railroad station in Paris—a newspaper writer called it the "Station of Ys"—and lapped at the foundation of Notre Dame Cathedral. And it's about the fearsome ruined abbey H. G. Wells saw in his undersea story "In the Abyss," and about Swinburne's crumbling, wave-gnawed cathedral town of Dunwich—Debussy admired Swinburne, who was translated by his friend Gabriel Mourey and championed by his friend Pierre Louÿs—and about the watery bells in Brahms's lost city of Vineta. And it's about Gerhart Hauptmann's *Sunken Bell*, and about Verlaine's and Huysmans's cathedrals, and about the *"ville disparu"* in Victor Hugo's *Légende des Siècles* and the underwater reef with "the sublimity of the cathedral" in Hugo's *Toilers of the Sea*. And it's about the article Proust wrote for *Le Figaro* on the death of the cathedrals. If France's cathedrals were allowed to fall into ruin, Proust wrote in 1904, the country would be like a beach strewn with giant empty shells. It's about the loss of nineteenth-century certainties. It's about all these things. And it's about Chopin's preludes, too, which were submerged and dissolved and remade by Debussy, with new harmonic flavors and fragrances, and it's about the two operas that Debussy knew he would never finish, one based on the Tristan story, and one based on Poe's "Fall of the House of Usher," and it's about the Gothic arches of the inner harp of the piano that he knows he can't play forever—the black box of hammers that outlives the hammerer. It's about death and what survives death. It's about burial at sea. It's about all the plans and loves and flaxen-haired singers of Debussy's idle youth that are now no more. It's about the time he and his friend Gabriel Pierné cut out pictures from a bound edition of *Le Monde Illustré* and put them up in his room. It's about the time that Debussy and his wife, Emma, and their young daughter, wearing a big floppy hat, had a wicker-basket picnic in dappled woods. It's about morphine and despair and undersea sponges and the long-gone days of focused effort when he was a soon-to-be father composing *La Mer*. It's about wanting to be a young prizewinning improvisational genius again, and knowing that this moment in C major was the best he could do now. Debussy didn't normally write in the key of C major. He chose C major this time, I think, because C is like water, clear and simple and bright and transparent, composed entirely of white keys, but if you hold down the pedal and play the clear white notes together in a certain way, the sound becomes blurred and pale blue and lost in haze, like a distant monument seen through water. He swam closer toward the cathedral, and its image became more clearly defined, with pounding, towering, unblurred C major chords, until he reached middle C, or middle sea. That's what the sunken cathedral is—it's the piano of his whole life.

ON MONDAY I woke up feeling dull and lost, as sometimes happens on Mondays, and I drove to Stockbridge, Massachusetts, where "The Sunken Cathedral" was first performed in the United States a little more than a hundred years ago, on July 26, 1910. The pianist was Walter Morse Rummel, a then famous songwriter who was the grandson of the inventor of the telegraph. Also on the program—I guess it was a long evening—were some Chopin pieces, some Couperin, some Handel, Rummel's own piano sonata "To a

Memory," and two compositions by Edward MacDowell, "From a Wandering Iceberg" and "To the Sea." Rummel was Debussy's favorite pianist. Once Debussy wrote Rummel a praising letter, in his tiny, almost indecipherable handwriting, about a performance Rummel had given. "One doesn't congratulate the sea for being more beautiful than cathedrals," he said.

I got to Stockbridge at about noon, and after a lot of GPS'ing and driving around—always being careful to use my turn signal—I found the former Casino building where Rummel had played. In the twenties the building was moved to a quieter place out of town, and it's now the main stage of the Berkshire Theatre Festival. It was designed by Stanford White. This was where the cathedral first submerged itself in the United States. I looked at the white building from the car for a while, parked near a young birch tree, and I ate a carrot and felt very little emotion. Then I climbed a set of steps to a permanently locked door. Its windows were covered with a layer of rubberized diffuser, painted black, as were the three large arched windows on the front façade. They wanted it dark inside. An abandoned wasps' nest was tucked into the doorway's lower left corner. I took some pictures and got back in the car. I considered putting on my headphones and listening again to Paul Jacobs play "The Sunken Cathedral," to beef up the occasion, but the building had been moved, after all. You have to choose your sunken occasions carefully.

Instead I read an interview that Debussy gave to a woman from *The New York Times* that same summer of 1910, soon after he had himself first performed "The Sunken Cathedral" and three other of the preludes in Paris. Debussy, who was wearing a blue suit, left the Blüthner piano when the interviewer arrived and sat at his desk, which was immaculate except for a few ink stains on the blotter. The interviewer asked him how he composed. Debussy said that he really didn't know how to explain it. He had to begin with a subject, he said. He concentrated on the subject for a while. "Gradually after these thoughts have simmered for a certain length of time music begins to centre around them, and I feel that I must give expression to the harmonies which haunt me. And then I work unceasingly."

Did he always like music? the interviewer asked. Yes, he was always fond of music, he said, although he was no child prodigy. He didn't always agree with what he was taught at the Conservatory, but he kept his opinions to himself— he wanted to graduate. He didn't care for genres and classifications—he just wanted music to be beautiful. "Beauty in a woman—and in music—is a great deal, a very great deal."

I banged the steering wheel. Right on, Claude! I kept reading. He said he couldn't live up to the ideals he tried to put into his music. "I feel the difference there is in me, between Debussy, the composer, and Debussy, the man. And so, you see, from its very foundations, art is untrue. Everything about it is an illusion, a transposition of facts." The interviewer disagrees. By the end of the article it's clear that she—I think it's a she, I think it's a writer named Emilie

Bauer—has fallen in love with Debussy. "He spoke with such warmth," she writes, "he was so carried away, that one felt how the work of the French composer is exactly a reproduction of his soul—a sensitive, delicate soul, yet determined and firm."

I turned on the ignition and drove home a different way, and here's what I saw: town, town, town, town, town, town. None of the towns made sense anymore because the needs that had brought them into being as towns were no longer needs. The flow of the river, the spire of the church, the little cluster of stores, they were none of them important. What lasted was the clustering itself—the grouping of houses and the fiction of the center of town, and then the miracle mile outside town where people really shopped. The supermarket with the bakery in it with passable octopus muffins that killed the real bakery. I drove by the abandoned road that led down to the lost town of Enfield, flooded in the forties during the building of the Quabbin Reservoir. I got some gas in a convenience store and went inside to buy a bag of salted almonds. A kid of maybe eighteen was walking around the store with his mother, cracking his knuckles. He was one of the loudest knuckle-crackers I've ever heard. He had a gift for it. The sound was like those clacking balls that were in vogue for a while when I was in grade school. He held one hand up, as if to support a violin, and with the other hand he bent his thumb back, and then bent his finger, and from his hands came a ghastly clacking. I stared openly at him and he ignored me, and I realized that like me he was doing his best to let the world know that he existed. I drove off toward New Hampshire, thinking maybe I should rent a bassoon and start playing again. Then I thought of the ache in my jaw. Goodbye, bassoon.

ON ROUTE 16, I saw a yellow banner on the back of a truck that said OVERSIZE LOAD. I turned on my recorder. "He was driving down the road with an oversize load," I sang.

> It was big
> It was bad
> It was round
> It could explode
>
> Yeah, he was driving down the road
> With an oversize load.

I remembered a talk I'd gone to at the University of New Hampshire once. Rebecca Rule, who is Portsmouth's jolly postmistress of literature, was in conversation with Charles Simic onstage. Simic hadn't yet been appointed Poet Laureate back then. He read a poem by a Serbian poet named Vasko Popa, part of the poet's "little box" series. Poets sometimes write a series of poems on one subject. Ted Hughes did it with *Crow*, the book he published after his wife Sylvia Plath killed herself, which has frightening Leonard Baskin illustrations. I tried to do it with my flying spoon poems but I finished only one of them. Vasko Popa's poem was a story about a little box that grew and swallowed up the cabinet that it, or she—she was a female box—was in. She got bigger and then the room was inside her, and then the house, and then the town, and then the whole world. And now there's a little box that you can put in your pocket that holds everything. It's easy to lose it. "Take care of the little box" is the last line of the poem.

I passed the truck, which was carrying half of a modular house. The driver had an elbow on the door. He was relaxed. He knew his job. Ahead of us there was some slow traffic and the driver pulled on his jake brake for a moment. He pulled it almost lovingly. And I suddenly understood about jake brakes.

A jake brake is a method of somehow using the truck's compressed air system to slow the truck down, rather than using the friction on the brake shoes. It makes a blatting, flatulent sound. The faster the truck is going, the louder the flatulence. And I knew that this driver was in the trucking business partly because he liked jake brakes. They made a lot of noise, and they sounded like motorcycles, and they were basically a way of having a wonderful huge powerful trumpeting farting sound emanating from where you were.

What the driver of the oversize load wanted was not that different from what I wanted. He wanted to make a sound. He wanted to have people hear him. This truck was his medium. This was how he sang. Some people sing through motorcycles and wear T-shirts that say "Loud Pipes Save

Lives," some sing with a guitar, some people crack their knuckles loudly.

When I got home I opened a letter from the IRS and read it. They were losing patience with me. I thought, This is dumb. I need fifteen hundred dollars right now. I called up a man I know at one of the boatyards in Kittery and asked him if they needed help shrink-wrapping boats. I knew they would, and they did. I've done it before during times of economic hardship. It's satisfying work, better than painting houses because the ladders are shorter. You haul a sheet of white plastic off a large roller and drape it over a big boat called, for instance, *Cookie's Dream*, whose owner can't afford to keep it afloat, and then you pass a flaming wand over the plastic, not too close, so that it shrinks to the hull's curve and the form of the frame that you've built over the deck, and in the end you have made an enormous white lumpy anonymous shape that sits outside in a boat parking lot with many other white anonymous shapes. The boatyard plays an oldies station on the radio, and they pay in cash. There are a lot of boats in the tall weeds out back, even in high summer, because so many people are out of money. Occasionally the owners return and cut away some of the plastic and have picnics on their stored boats, or play poker.

Thirty-two

I CALLED ROZ'S NUMBER and she answered. I asked if she was hungry.

"Yes!" she said.

"Because I have a fresh tank of hummus and some pita chips. Chickpeas are supposed to be good for you. They have lots of iron."

"I'd love some hummus."

"When should I come over?"

"Now is good."

There was traffic on the highway and I was late getting there. Lucy let me in and greeted Smack, who wagged his tail wildly. Roz was in her bedroom, propped slightly on pillows. The room, which was white, with blue trim around the windows, had the quiet, almost sacred feeling of convalescence.

"It's good to see you," Roz said. "Pardon my state of

dishevelment. Thank you for the Mary Oliver, and the music."

I opened the bag and gave her a chip. She dipped it into the hummus.

"Wow, this is so delicious," she said. "Wow, wow, wow." She adjusted herself in the bed and winced. "I'm hugely bloated. My insides have expanded to fill the void."

I said I figured they had some adjusting to do.

"They certainly do," she said. "But everything seems to have worked out. Modern medicine, you know? When it's good, it's good."

She asked me what I was doing, and I told her I'd put in some afternoons of shrink-wrapping at the boatyard and that my arms were sore. And that I'd written a dance song using some of the three-word phrases she'd sent. And that I'd spent the afternoon in the parking lot while she had her operation.

"That's good of you. You're a good man."

"A good man needs a good woman. How is Dr. Harris? Is he the man?"

She patted my hand to silence me. "I've been thinking about a lot of things," she said. "Ellen, my gynecologist, believes in Reiki massage."

"Oh, heavens."

"No, no, it was good. Before the operation, they put me in an enormous hospital bathrobe and took me into a very dim room and I sat in a comfortable chair, and a woman came in with a portable kind of boom box that was playing, I guess, Reiki massage music. The woman was all in black, except for some turquoise jewelry, and she held her hands for a long time on my shoulders, then on my hips, then on my stomach, then on my feet. It was so soothing. She said, 'Think of me as a cord that goes from the music to you.' She said the music was from Tibet, and that it was two thousand years old. She said we had places in our bodies where the energy can get stuck, and that she was going to release the energy so that it could flow freely. It sounds very New Agey, but I just sat there with my eyes closed feeling peaceful, and my mind suddenly filled with happy memories of walking with you and the dear dog at Fort McClary. They were such good memories."

"I'm glad," I said.

"And then she went away and Ellen came back and touched my arm and said, 'How are you, any questions?' I said, 'No, I'm sorry, I don't have any questions—this is so peaceful I find that I'm crying.' And I wiped my eyes on the sleeve of my bathrobe and felt grateful. And then I had the operation, and I spent the night in a room with a very loud grouchy woman who moaned and farted all night long, and I've been in sort of a fog since. I've been listening to the music you gave me. Tell me about that Brazilian piece in which the woman sings."

"Bachianas Brasileiras," I said. "She's singing about the moon. My dad used to play it for me, and I thought you'd like it." Then the doorbell buzzed. Smack barked furiously. He's vigilant about doorbells. I looked at Roz.

"Oops, that may be him," she whispered.

"I better go," I said.

"I'll talk to you soon."

Harris had arrived bearing a ceramic pot of flowers wrapped in plastic. We shook hands coolly.

"I'm just on my way out," I said, waving. "Bye-bye."

TODAY'S SECRET WORD is "garbanzo." A very warm and nauseatingly friendly hello to you all on this tender summer day. You may be interested in "the poet's day," aka my day.

I opened my eyes this morning and I saw that the sky was blue, with two clouds shaped like ZiL limousines waiting for passengers near the horizon, and I saw that there were some cable TV lines outside the window. The cable lines were no surprise, because they've been there for many years now. All the cable companies string their wires along the same upright wooden bar lines, as if they're trying to write a song.

I lay in bed blinking and thinking. The dream I'd just had was about finding an old bicycle horn on a shadowy set of subway stairs somewhere near Columbia. The blue rubber bulb was faded and cracked but the horn still croaked. The stairs were covered in old, slippery magazines and trash— the footing was dangerous. I put the bicycle horn in my pocket and made my way carefully down to the noise and heat of the station. In the back of my copy of Tony Hoagland's *What Narcissism Means to Me* I wrote a note about my dream, and I read one of Hoagland's poems, "How It Adds Up." He says that he listened once through a door as someone, "obviously not me," made love to his girlfriend.

I went downstairs and pushed the button on the coffee machine, and I opened the door so that the morning air could come in through the screen, and I fed the dog and let him out. He found his place under the car, where he's dug a low, cool spot for himself in the driveway sand. He sits there for hours sometimes. He's getting older.

I put a waffle in the toaster and ate it, with some local maple syrup from an unbeautiful beige plastic jug, and thought—not for the first time—that what I should really do with my life is be a designer of syrup jugs for all the maple syrup boiler-downers who live around here. Surely there's a better color of plastic jug than beige. There's a maple farm in Alfred, Maine, that makes an exceptional dark amber syrup that's enough to make you throw your arms out and thank the fates for this concoction, which is better than laudanum and better than morphine. Better than Yukon Jack, almost. It's similar in a way to Yukon Jack in that it's sweet and viscous.

I rinsed off the plate and put it in the dishwasher and thought that tonight I might run the dishwasher. I run a load every three or four days, so it's a big deal for me. Then I wrote a fast loop with a massive kick drum from the Deep House Kit and a Round Reggae Organ doing karate chops up on top. First I tried singing, "I've figured out—what I'm going to do." I scrapped that and sang, "He's no good for you, he's no good for you." That worked better. The man across the street began chainsawing a tree, which interfered with my recording, so I closed all the windows, imagining what people would say if I ever had a dance club hit: "And he recorded it all at his kitchen table!" The refrigerator hum bothered me while I was singing, so I used a quarter to turn its thermostat off, and when I did I remembered how much Roz had liked the hummus.

Hummus is made of chickpeas, plus a lot of garlic. And then I thought: garbanzo beans. Chickpeas are garbanzo beans. Garbanzo, garbanzo, garbanzo! It's a great word partly because it has a slight suggestion of garbage in it, garbage gone gonzo, and yet it's not garbage at all, it's a bean. It's a living edible bean that some call a chickpea. Sometimes you're in the mood for a short, peckish, two-syllable word, "chickpea," and sometimes you're in the mood for a long, suggestive word like "garbanzo." It's all a matter of mood.

I spent fifteen minutes trying to substitute "garbanzo" for "Guantanamo" in the Guantanamo song. I'd like to say it was a perfect fit, but it wasn't. I sang, "Wash it away." And then, "Dance it away." Then, "Rinse it away." Then I went back to "Wash it away." "Wash" is a good word. Sometimes you're in the mood for a word like "wash." There's a part of England that's called the Wash—a low area on the east coast where the ocean washed over the land before they lured in the Dutch engineers in the seventeenth century and built the dikes. The past washes over all of us. And when it washes over us, it comes and it goes. It's a palindrome of oceanic activity.

I've got a headache now, frankly, and I'm out of Faustos. I'm reduced to smoking a mild no-name cigar from a sample pack, and it's just not the same. If you're going to smoke a cigar, you might as well smoke a dark one from Nicaragua that really smacks your brain.

Thirty-three

I'VE BEEN SHRINK-WRAPPING in the afternoons. It's hard work, and I've slowed down a bit with the songwriting. I did make part of a short one. Raymond sent me a toothsome bassline and some beats and I added chords on the Talky Klav and some Middle Eastern sounds using a plug-in I've discovered called Alchemy. A plug-in is a whole separate piece of software, with its own samples, that works inside Logic. Alchemy has some exotic instruments, including one that's halfway between a harp and a xylophone, and a whole set called Steamworx made by a sound designer, Martin Walker, who sampled an old clock and his dog's water bowl and many proto-industrial sounds of rending and crunching and letting off steam. In an instrument called Churchyard, Walker includes a note: "An entire horror film soundtrack could be played with this preset!" But I wasn't interested in making a horror film soundtrack, no, thank you. What I wanted, as always, I guess, was to write a love song. My chorus goes, "I'm curious, just a bit curious, whether fate will hurry us, to a nice place." Raymond said kind things about it, although it isn't exactly his sort of music. He really is a great kid, and it's a completely different feeling to be writing a song with the help of another person.

This morning, Jeff and his crew were working on the new floor to the barn and they made a lot of noise. They left at about eleven, and in the beautiful quiet I made another mix of "Take a Ride in My Boat" and of "Marry Me," panning the instruments to the right and left for a good stereo effect. I smoked two Faustos and a Bone Crusher and felt burpy and sick and burned a hole in my pants. Then I spent an afternoon at the boatyard and got paid. I drove to Kittery Trading Post and walked up and down the racks of canoes. There was a new red Old Town canoe marked down because it had a minor scratch. I bought it, along with two new orange life jackets, and strapped it on my Kia.

At six I called up Roz to find out how she was.

"I'm having my staples out tomorrow," she said. "Ellen the gynecologist is going to be paying a house call!"

"And you feel good?"

"I'm much more mobile. I can make it from the bed to the bathroom in under five minutes."

"Great. Listen, I have three questions for you. The first one is, I found a book of yours in the bookcase. It's *The*

Genius, by Theodore Dreiser. Do you want it or should I keep it here for you?"

There was a brief, complicated silence. "You keep it there, I think."

"I read a little of it, something about a faded crumpled memory of a hat. It was pretty good."

"I'm glad you're reading it."

"And the second question is—do you want to go dancing with me at Stripe?"

"What's Stripe?"

"It's a dance club, right here downtown on Chapel Street." I told her that Nan's son Raymond was DJ'ing there soon and that Nan and her boyfriend Chuck were going to hear him. "You wouldn't have to dance, obviously," I said. "But if you're feeling mobile already, maybe by then you'd like to get out into the world and do something. I don't think you ever met Chuck."

"I don't think I did," Roz said.

"Anyway, we wouldn't stay long. We'd just sit and be supercool older people and take in the ambience. I'll bring the sunglasses."

"That's a nice invitation—" Roz didn't say anything for a while.

"It might be fun," I said. "Raymond's going to be playing some of his songs and remixes, and he says he might play something that he and I worked on together. I used the words that you sent me in it. It's called 'Take a Ride in My Boat.'

You didn't know you wrote a song, did you?—but you did. So do you want to go with me?"

"Sure, I guess. It depends on how I'm feeling. But yes, if I can."

"Great. And the third question is, Can I come over tonight and hear about your lurid Vicodin dreams?"

"Oh, you don't want to hear about those—just a lot of group groping in trees. And tonight isn't so good, because Lucy's moving back to her own place tomorrow and this is our last dinner together. She's been an incredible help, but she needs to sleep in her own bed. So I'll be on my own tomorrow. You could come by after I've gotten my staples out."

"Will Harris suddenly show up with a potted plant?"

"No chance of that, he's in Washington. There's a big pharmaceutical conference where he's planning to ask some awkward questions. Come by tomorrow."

WIKIPEDIA HAS a short article on Tibetan music, which seems to have influenced Philip Glass's soundtrack to *Kundun*. I listened to some of *Kundun* and then I listened to a man in Tucson bang Tibetan bowls and blow on his didgeridoo. It probably wasn't at all like what Roz had heard during her Reiki massage, but it wasn't bad. I made some more adjustments to my songs and burned a CD of them. I emailed one of the songs, the one about the right of the people to peaceable assembly, to Tim, and I called the boatyard to say I couldn't do any shrink-wrapping that afternoon. After de-cigarring myself thoroughly, I drove Smacko to Concord. I opened Roz's door a bit and called her name.

"Up here!" she said. She was sitting in bed, watching *Judge Judy*. "Please don't look at me, I'm a mess."

"You look pretty."

"No I don't, but Judge Judy is fascinating."

"She's full of wisdom," I said.

"She gets to the heart of the problem fast," said Roz. "This one's about a hit-and-run. That's the boyfriend." We watched Judge Judy look at a photograph of a car and pepper the plaintiff with pertinent questions. Then a commercial for dryer sheets came on and Roz turned off the TV. The dog had found some of her dirty laundry and was napping contentedly on it. "So what's been going on? Tell me everything."

"Did I tell you that Tim got arrested at a drone protest in Syracuse?"

"No. Tim is unstoppable. He's impressive. I wish he'd stayed together with Hannah."

I asked her if the gynecologist had come and taken out her staples.

"She did indeed," said Roz. "She came and she was very chatty and proud of her handiwork. She said I was doing well."

"Are you?"

Roz pushed at her pillows. "Well, Harris and I are taking

a little break. We had a very long, very exhausting talk—he's a talker—and I think it's for the best. He wasn't terribly happy about running into you here."

"Oh, geez. Jealous." I pulled my chair closer to the bed.

"Jealous, and just not—not—not what the doctor ordered. Speaking of which, can you help me with something? I need you to put my mind at ease."

"Tell me," I said, leaning forward.

"Here's the situation. It feels like Ellen maybe forgot something. I was telling her about the book you gave me, the Mary Oliver book—I loaned it to her, I hope that's all right."

Of course, I said.

"I love the poem about the deer. Anyway, she got so interested in talking about all the poetry that she'd read in college, and how she wants to read more, and doesn't have time to read, and on and on, that, I think she maybe, um—"

"What?"

"Didn't take out all the staples." She reached under her sheet, looking around the room as she felt for something with her fingers. "I think I feel one right at the edge of the incision. But maybe not. Maybe it's just an illusion. Maybe it's just the edge of where they cut. It's still quite numb down there. But it really feels like a staple."

"Mm," I said. "You should call her and ask her to come back."

"I don't want to call her. What if there's no staple there?"

I waited, then said, "Do you want me to look?"

"No, because it's a disgusting incision, but yes. If you could just put my mind at rest that all the staples are gone."

"Happy to do it. Should I do it now?"

"Let me get arranged. Turn around for a second. I need to maintain what's left of my modesty."

I turned around while Roz adjusted the bedclothes.

"That's the best I can do," she said. When I turned back, she had folded the sheet back and tucked it around her hips, leaving a bit of herself exposed. "It's this place right here," she said.

I knelt by the bed and looked at her pale skin and the very white and pink healing scar where the surgeon had cut. I was surprised that they'd been able to get Roz's whole uterine fibroid complex out through a cut that size. I could see two rows of tiny holes where the staples had been, and there were still traces of yellow antiseptic on the thin-lipped incision. "It's discreet," I said.

"Not all that discreet, but she told me that if they'd waited any longer they would have had to cut this way, up and down, and I didn't want that."

"No, you never want that," I said.

"Two pounds of meat came out of me. A real Sunday roast."

"Jesus, Roz. It looks like it's healing well."

"Yes, but could you just have a look right—here." She tapped a place on the end of the wound.

I looked. "It's red and it's a little swollen," I said. Then I saw a glint of something silver. "You're right, there's a staple right in here. It's sort of hidden. It's right here!"

"Dang, I knew it."

"You should call Ellen. She should come back and take it out."

"I guess I should. I really don't want to, though. It'll embarrass her. She'll know she messed up."

"Well, she sort of did."

Roz looked at me and raised an eyebrow. "The staple remover is just over there," she said. She pointed to a plastic bag on a side table near a lamp. I went over to it.

In the bag was some gauze, a tool that looked like a hole puncher, and about twenty bent staples. I looked at the tool and at the bent staples. I whistled.

"What do you think?" Roz said.

"About taking out your staple? I guess I could give it a try. But I'm worried I'd do it wrong and maybe hurt you."

"It's not that hard. I watched her do it. I thought it would hurt, but it didn't. She was chatting away."

"Yes, but she removes staples all the time. She's a trained professional."

"And yet she missed one."

I decided I really had to step up to the plate. "Let me practice first," I said. I fished out one of the staples from the bag and used my fingers to bend it to its original angular C shape, so that the V-shaped kink in its back was gone. Then, holding it in the air, I gave it a trial pinch with the staple remover. The two staple ends lifted. It didn't seem too hard. It certainly wasn't as difficult as pulling a staple out of a piece of paper. I washed my hands in the bathroom. Over the towel holder was a woodblock print of three eggs in a nest.

I went back to the bed and knelt. "You ready?"

"I'm ready."

I steadied my arm on Roz's leg and took a breath. "Here goes." I angled the machine so that the tiny pointed nippers were over and under the visible silver segment of staple. "Does that hurt?" I said.

"No."

I squeezed. "I'm squeezing now," I said. "Does that hurt?"

"Nope."

I squeezed some more. The staple bent upward and its sharp edges withdrew from Roz's soft, vulnerable skin. Her sheet had shifted a little and I could see the edge of her pubic hair. It wasn't a sexual thing—it was just a part of the whole experience.

"Got it!" I said.

"Ah, how wonderful," said Roz, pulling up the sheet. She put her hand on her chest. "Relief."

I put the last staple in the bag. "The offending scrap of metal is officially gone," I said. I noticed my hand was trembling.

"Now I'll stop fretting," Roz said. "Thank you for all your help. You've been a wonderful, dear person through this whole ordeal."

"Nothing to it," I said. "My pleasure. And I have another question for you. Would you like to get married? Because I think it's time."

"Oh, baby—that's very nice of you."

"Don't say no yet, I'm just throwing it out there. I know it's abrupt. I don't have any Reiki music for you, but I'll play you a song."

"One of your songs?"

I slid the CD in her clock radio. "It's still rough. Forgive the intonation." I hit Play. Two Indian bansuri flutes came on, playing in parallel thirds at a hundred beats per minute, with some skipping high hat and a few chords on the Mark II keyboard. Then I heard myself singing:

I saw you and thought you looked very nice
You said you had other places to be
We went to a restaurant
Had a salad or two
Talked about some things
And found out what we wanted to do

Spent more time together
In the library and out in the town
Went to a dance
But the music was way too loud

Oh it was fun
To be with you
Oh it was fun
To be with you

Mine was mine and yours was truly yours
Then we ate some cake and shared it with two forks

Nobody was able to take us from each other
And then one day we woke up under the same cover

Oh it was fun
To be with you
Oh it was fun
To be with you

Maybe you think I'm being premature
I've had trouble with that in the past for sure

But I know that it's time
To pop that question
Rhyme it up in rhyme

Isn't it time that you and I should marry
I really don't want you going out with Dick and Harry

Find your shoes
Walk the walk
Get plenty of sleep
Don't eat the chalk

There's lots to do
Plenty to see
And that's why you
Should get married to me

When it was over, Roz sat smiling at me.

"So, what do you think?" I said. I held her hand. "Should I kneel?"

"You already did that when you took out my staple."

"That's true."

Roz said, "I think it's a lovely song. I think it's a lovely idea, too, and I love you, but I have to get better first. I have to be thinking clearly."

"Clear thinking is overrated," I said.

"I know, but a lot has happened."

"That's true. Well, give it some consideration. I'll leave you with the CD. If you feel up to a dance club with loud music and gyrating bodies, we can go and talk more then."

"Thank you, Pauly. You're a dear man."

We kissed awkwardly—I didn't want to jostle her in bed.

I drove home thinking, Holy shit, I took out her staple. I have work to do in this world. Even if she decides not to marry me, that was a good moment. It was the best moment of the day.

Thirty-four

O N SUNDAY BY MISTAKE I closed the door on the cord from my headphones and drove to Quaker meeting with it dragging on the road. I kept hearing little sounds coming from outside the car, but I thought it was just pebbles from my tires. But no, it was the tip of my headphone cord. The stereo plug was ground down to a sharp point, and when I plugged it into my iPhone I got only the left channel. Doesn't matter. It's just a pair of headphones. It gives me an excuse to go to Best Buy and have a close look at the Korg Kaossilator.

In Quaker meeting a woman was knitting something brown and red as the clock ticked. She was a very quiet knitter, but I could hear her needles click and slide against each other. Out of the corner of my eye, I watched her fingers form quick loops of yarn and do things with them. Across the room, Chase stood and said that he'd read something adapted from Proverbs: "Once our eyes are opened, we can't pretend we don't know what to do." He sat down. I thought of the misery hat, which is something you knit for yourself and all of a sudden you're wearing it. I thought, I can't, I'm sorry, Gene. I can't keep from wearing the misery hat sometimes. I remembered Roya, the girl in Afghanistan whose father gathered parts of his wife and his sons from the trees by his house. Roya lived through something inconceivable. She survived, but barely. And my job was to think about her, right then, because we were responsible. We did this to Roya— with our missiles, our taxes, our Air Force, our targeters, our elected government. We exported a war into her young life. I thought, What can I possibly do to help Roya and her father? And the answer was: Nothing. There was nothing I could do. I considered standing in meeting and saying this, but it didn't feel right, and I'd spoken recently. I shook hands and told Chase that I was grateful to him for his message, and I went outside and sat in my car for twenty minutes, and then I drove home and began making a song out of piano and Turkish oud and the Alchemy plug-in and percussion. The only thing I could do that had any possible meaning was to write a short, inadequate piece of music about the missile attack that destroyed Roya's life.

And that's what I did. I wrote a two-minute song with one word in it: Roya. I put fear in it and panic, and I sang Roya's name several times at the end. I tried to put the imagined insanity to a beat. The song will not help her. It's not a comforting song. It's not a good song. But it is a way of remembering. It's a way of paying attention to a single event by surrounding it with many notes. The notes point like arrows to the wrong.

And then I took off the misery hat and gently put it away in a box.

Thirty-five

I RODE IN THE BACK SEAT with Nan and Chuck and we met Roz and Lucy outside Stripe's secret striped door. Roz was still pale and moving carefully, but she'd put on makeup and she was wearing a black tank top and looked gloriously bosomy, if I may be forgiven the impertinence. I introduced Lucy and everyone said hello. Roz took my arm. "You look wonderful," I said. "We'll just stay for a short time. Let me know if you want to go."

I tried to pay the cover charge, but Chuck brought out his wallet and insisted on doing it—let him spend his nuclear money, I thought—and we bought drinks. The place was not full, but there were people dancing and the music was loud. We sat at the bar: five middle-aged people in a place that wasn't really meant for them. Raymond was up on a low platform, his headphoned head bobbing like crazy. When he saw us, he waved at us in a cool, low-handed way. Nan beamed. I didn't recognize the music. Then I did: Raymond played "Amsterdam" by Paul Oakenfold. "I love this song!" I said. Roz was moving to the beat. She hadn't forgotten how to dance. And Raymond queued something up and the song that he and I had done together came on and I just about shat. I heard myself over the loudspeakers singing "Take a Ride in My Boat." And the incredible thing was, people kept dancing. They thought it was an actual song. Thank God for pitch correction software, I thought. I gave Raymond a thumbs-up sign.

It was almost too loud to talk, but Roz pointed at me with a questioning expression and I nodded. I held her shoulders and I shouted in her ear, "Your words helped!"

"Glad to hear it!" she shouted. "Raymond has really grown up!" Then Diplo's "Express Yourself" came on, and Nan and Chuck danced. Someone asked Lucy to dance and she went out with him. She was a good dancer, in a red-haired, embarrassed, happy sort of way. Raymond played his "Promises Burn" and people liked it, and after that "Sexual Healing" came on. Roz and I shouted bits of conversation about how much Lucy and Nan and Chuck were enjoying themselves, and we drank sips of Irish whiskey. It wasn't Tyrconnell, but it was good. And then, tentatively, we kissed. We were shy with each other, and it was a somewhat dry, sphinctery kiss—too public. I pointed to a side room where it was quieter and there was a comfortable couch with nobody on it.

"It's so good to see you," I said.

"It's good to see you. I liked the song, too. I'm not sure about 'Milk the meat,' though."

"I know, it's too much. I'm just glad you're here."

Roz held me and put her head in my neck, and I smelled her hair just the way I used to. I felt like crying and apologizing for all the wrong things I'd ever done, but instead I cleared my throat and said, "Just so you know, I'm done with cigars for the time being. Although I have to say they were very helpful."

"That's a relief. I was worried about that cough."

"I love you," I said. And then we kissed again, and it was a whole different sort of kiss this time. Our mouths remembered what they had to say to each other, and Roz's lips were, whoa mercy, so absolutely full and givingly soft and livingly true to her inmost infinite lovingkindness. Her kiss was like a lip life raft that was carrying us somewhere impossibly good.

"Allstate bought you new canoe," I said.

"How nice of them," she said. "Do you want to take a ride in my boat?"

I said I did, and we held each other for a long time. Then I drove her home.

Nicholson Baker is the author of nine novels, including *The Anthologist*, *Vox*, and *The Fermata*, and five works of nonfiction, including *Human Smoke* and *Double Fold* (winner of the National Book Critics Circle Award). He lives in Maine with his family.